Signs of Love

Stupid Cupid

Melody James

SIMON AND SCHUSTER

First published in Great Britain in 2012 by Simon and Schuster UK Ltd
A CBS COMPANY

Copyright © HotHouse Fiction Limited 2012

1 3 5 7 9 10 8 6 4 2

Simon & Schuster UK Ltd
1st Floor, 222 Gray's Inn Road
London
WC1X 8HB

Simon & Schuster Australia, Sydney

Simon & Schuster India, New Delhi

A CIP catalogue record for this book
is available from the British Library.

PB ISBN 978-0-85707-324-2
eBook ISBN 978-0-85707-325-9

Printed and bound by CPI Group (UK) Ltd, Croydon, CR0 4YY

www.simonandschuster.co.uk
www.simonandschuster.com.au
www.signs-of-love.co.uk

SIGNS of Love

With thanks to Kate Cary

'This is the worst dilemma ever!' Treacle drops her book bag on to my bedroom floor and starts pacing up and down. 'Do I go fashionista or frump?'

I flip on the light to banish the after-school gloom. 'Just wear something comfortable.' I start emptying homework from bag to bed, acting casual. Treacle has no idea that I have a surprise for her hidden in my wardrobe. I tighten my lips to stop a smile escaping.

'*Comfortable?*' Treacle winds a strand of her glossy black hair round a frantic finger. 'For me? Or Jeff? Or *them?*'

'*Them*' are Jeff's parents. Treacle's been invited to their house for tea. It will be her first meeting with Jeff's ancestors and she's not nervous, she's cup-final-at-Wembley *terrified*.

'You must have *something* suitable,' I reason calmly.

Treacle stops mid-pace. 'How do I know what's *suitable?*' she squawks. 'I've never *met* them! Their idea of *suitable* might be corsets and a tiara.'

'Have you asked Jeff?'

Treacle's fast-breathing. 'He just says "be yourself".' She starts fanning her eyes with hummingbird hands. She's welling up. 'But I have no idea who "myself" is!'

'You're *Treacle*!' I throw my arms round her. In the month since she started dating Jeff, my best friend has embraced her inner girl like a jackpot winner embracing a quiz show host. She's changed from hardcore footballer to Disney princess – but she still carries a pair of muddy football boots in her backpack and she's only a changing room away from her soccer jersey and a pair of stinking sports socks. I squeeze her harder. 'And that means you're fabulous and Jeff is lucky to have you as a girl-friend.'

'Really?' She looks at me with hopeful puppy-dog eyes.

'Really.' I nod decisively and head for my wardrobe. The smile's back on my lips, pushing the corners of my mouth wide as I reach through the crush of clothes and drag out a hanger.

A neat, tweed suit hangs from it like knitted moss. Pale green, knee-length, gold buttons, square jacket. It is *the* perfect meet-the-parents ensemble. I had to fight off a gaggle of pension-book fashionistas to grab this outfit in Oxfam.

'Ta-da!' I hold it up for Treacle to admire. 'As soon as I saw it in the charity shop, I thought of your visit with Jeff's old folk!'

Treacle's mouth is open. She must be getting the full granny-aroma that's wafting from the tweed.

'Don't worry,' I reassure her. 'The lady behind the counter said it's been dry-cleaned and that a splash of perfume and fresh air will blow away the smell.'

'I-I don't know what to say,' Treacle stammers.

'Try it on.' I'm picking up a vibe that tells me Treacle's not that impressed by my carefully chosen outfit, but that's OK. We're trying to dress her for *parents*, not a rave.

Gingerly, Treacle takes the suit and lays it on my bed. As she peels off her school jumper and slips into the jacket, I duck out on to the landing and call down the stairs. 'Any crisps, Mum?'

Mum's chatting with my brother Ben in the kitchen. I can hear them laughing. Ben has cystic fibrosis and last month a dark cloud almost crushed our family when he was admitted to hospital fighting for every breath. He's OK now, thank goodness, and it's wall to wall sunshine most days.

'Crisps?' Mum echoes up the stairs. 'Hold on.'

A minute later, Ben appears at the foot of the stairs with a tray loaded with crisps, sandwiches and two glasses of milk.

I grin at him as he carries them carefully upstairs. Ben's seven years old and still pleased when he gets the chance to show how grown up and responsible he can be.

'Thanks, Ben.' I take the tray from him when he gets to the top. 'I appreciate it.' I plant a sloppy kiss on his head.

He shakes me off and gallops downstairs. I love it when he seems like a totally normal brother – like he's not actually ill and doesn't need heaps of physiotherapy to keep his lungs gunk-free, or medicine to fight off the constant threat of infection.

'Thanks, Mum!' I yell over the banister and barge back into the bedroom, the tray heavy in my hands.

Treacle's standing, neat as a pin in the pale green suit. 'The plan is to *meet* Jeff's mum,' she says accusingly, 'not *be* her!'

She does look mumsy; like a mini-politician. If I pinned a rosette to the sharp-cut collar, she'd probably win the next local election.

I slide the tray on to my desk. 'It's not bad,' I lie. 'OK, so it swallows your shape a bit—'

'Swallows my shape *a bit?*' Treacle's eyes pop. 'My waist has disappeared and I have *armpit* lumps. Who has armpit lumps? And the colour – the colour . . .' She runs out of words.

I circle her. 'It *is* kind of more cabbagey than I thought.' I don't tell her the colour of the tweed is high-lighting every greenish tone in her smooth olive skin.

'I look like a toad!' Treacle stares in dismay at the mirror.

4

'But a well-brought-up, respectable toad,' I encourage. Treacle cracks a smile.

'The sort of toad that parents would approve of,' I press.

'It *is* smart,' she concedes. 'I bet Georgina Robyn-Earle dresses like this on the weekends.'

G R-E is a Year Twelve. She's got her own pony and skis every Easter in the Pyrenees.

'Mrs Simpson.' Treacle fixes me with a mischievous look as she pretends I'm Jeff's mum. 'I've brought you some jam.' As she holds out an imaginary jar for me to take, she slips into a plummy lisp. 'Mummy's got so many gooseberries this year she doesn't know what to do with them.'

I take the invisible jam, joining in the game. 'Oh, Treacle, dear. How kind. It's so lovely to meet you. When Jeff said he was bringing home his girlfriend, I was frightened you'd be one of those ravers you see so much of on the television.'

Treacle widens her eyes. 'Oh, gosh no. I've never raved in my life. Nor do I intend to.'

'You're not one of those festival types?' I ask suspiciously. 'You don't spend the summer in a tent with your hair in dreadlocks, do you?'

'Sometimes we take a picnic to the gymkhana.' Treacle's holding back a giggle. I can see it in her eyes. 'There's nothing better than a potted crab sandwich in the back of the Land Rover.' She lifts a wilting hand and crosses to the bed on the balls of her feet, like Cinderella tiptoeing in glass slippers. I swallow back a squawk of laughter as she goes on. 'Last year at Ascot, Daddy forgot the icebox and Mummy had to drink warm gin from a teacup.'

'Watch out, dear!' As Treacle lowers herself daintily on to the bed, I dive and grab a pillow from behind her. 'You'll squash the Chihuahua.' I cradle the pillow-pooch in my arms. 'Dear little Bubbles. He's still recovering from when Jeff mistook him for a football and booted him over the fence.' I stroke the pillow lovingly, fighting back giggles. 'I think Jeff was practising goal kicks because poor Bubbles flew over three gardens before he landed in the Robinson's swimming pool.'

'Noooo!' Treacle explodes with laughter and slides off the bed with a thump. She clutches her sides helplessly. 'Stop!'

'Poor Bubby!' Hooting, I collapse beside her, the image of a low-flying Chihuahua fixed in my head.

As the giggles slowly ease, an idea sparks in my brain. 'Come on!' I sit up and tug her arm. 'Let's try it properly.'

'What?' Treacle looks puzzled. 'Booting a chihuahua?'

'No, idiot! Role-play! It'll give you chance to practise. No jokes this time. I'll pretend to be Jeff's mum.'

Treacle gives a nervous frown.

'Don't worry,' I reassure her. 'I'll be gentle.' I scramble

6

to my feet and straighten my skirt. 'Treacle dear.' I hold out a hand. 'How lovely to meet you. Jeff's talked about nothing else these past few weeks.'

'Really?' Treacle gets to her feet and tentatively takes my hand.

I shake it heartily. 'Absolutely! It's been "Treacle this, Treacle that" for weeks. Do you mind me calling you Treacle or would you rather I called you Tracy?'

'Um ... er ...' Treacle's eyes cloud with confusion.

'Tell her Treacle's fine,' I hiss, dropping out of character for a second.

'T-Treacle's fine,' she stammers.

'Good. Lovely. You can call me Mary.'

Treacle blinks. 'Is that her name?'

'It is now,' I answer briskly. 'Come and sit down.' I pat the bed and wait till Treacle takes a seat. Then I head for the tray. 'Would you like some milk, Treacle?' I lift a glass from the tray and offer it to her.

'I'm not really thirsty,' Treacle answers.

'Sandwich?'

Treacle shakes her head. 'Not hungry.'

'Really? A growing girl like you?' I grab a sandwich for myself and plump down next to Treacle on the bed. 'You're not one of those funny eaters, are you?'

Treacle shakes her head.

'Vegetarian?' I ask. 'We've a friend with a daughter who's just turned vegetarian. Poor things. They have to cook bean burgers every night. It's all she'll eat.' I take another bite of sandwich. Cheese and mustard. My favourite. 'Where do you live?'

'Mulberry Crescent.'

'Really?' I swallow. 'Which end? Crook Street or Tottington Avenue?'

Treacle rubs the side of her nose. 'Kind of in the middle.'

'Hmm.' I frown as I cram in the last of the sandwich. 'Are you sure you're not hungry? They're very good.'

'No thank you Mrs Simps—' Treacle corrects herself. '*Mary*. I ate before I came out.'

'Really?' I frown. Time to increase the pressure. 'Didn't Jeff tell you we'd be having dinner?'

Treacle looks flustered. 'Well, yes.'

'It seems a little thoughtless to eat beforehand.'

'I-I-er-I . . .'

While Treacle fishes for a reply, I push on. I'm really living the part now. Being a middle-aged bossy-boots is fun. 'Never mind. We can always donate what you don't need to the soup kitchen. I hear they're always in need.'

Treacle's twitching like a flustered terrier beside me. 'When I said I'd eaten, it was only a packet of crisps on the bus, I'm sure I'll be hungry in a minute. I'm just a bit nervous, that's all.'

'Nervous, dear?' I turn a spectacularly amazed look on

her. 'Of meeting *us*? Did Jeff tell you we're monsters or something?'

'No, no! Jeff didn't say anything.'

'Because if he did, I'd feel very disappointed in him.'

'Really—' Treacle balls her fists '—he didn't say anything.' I feel her fluster hardening into irritation, but I'm not turning down the heat. I want her to be prepared for anything.

'He didn't mention us *at all*?' I flash her a wounded look and then move on swiftly. 'So you play football?'

'Yes, for the school.'

'Jeff plays for the county.'

'I'm going to try out for the county team,' Treacle says quickly.

'That's nice, dear. But it's a lot of time and energy to devote to something that's not really going to take you anywhere.' As Treacle's eyes spark with indignation, I carry on. 'It's not like a girl could ever go on to play football professionally.' I know Treacle's got her whole footballing career mapped out, but Jeff's mum won't. 'Surely you'd be better off spending the time on schoolwork. Then you'll be able to get a nice little job as a secretary or something.'

'Secretary or something?' The spark in Treacle's eyes ignites into fury. 'This is the twenty-first century Mrs— Mary! Women become lawyers and surgeons and CEOs!'

'I'm pleased to hear you're aiming high but, once you marry and settle down, you'll want to put your family first, surely?'

Treacle leaps to her feet. 'Oh! My! God!' She's outraged. 'You want someone to cook and clean for your son and provide you with grandchildren? It's like one of those old books we read at school! There's no way I'm going to end up as a housewife.'

I gaze at her innocently. 'It's been a good enough career for me.'

'Really?' Treacle puts her hands on her hips. 'Well it's not good enough for me! You should be locked up somewhere in the nineteenth century where you belong! If you're looking for a nice little stay-at-home wife for your precious son, you'd better look somewhere else, because it's not going to be me, you stupid old bag!'

Her face is beetroot-red, her eyes wild. She looks so funny!

'Whoa! Treacle!' I laugh.

Treacle claps her hands over her mouth in horror. 'I just called Jeff's mum a stupid old bag!'

'Maybe save that for your second meeting,' I suggest.

'Why did you have to push me like that?' Treacle's puffing like an angry bull. 'Mrs Simpson's not going to be grilling me about marriage.'

I smile up at her sweetly. 'I just wanted to make sure you were prepared for anything.'

'*Gemma!*' Treacle grabs the pillow-pooch and starts bashing me furiously.

I burrow for cover under the duvet, laughing. 'Don't hurt poor Bubbles!'

'You're no help!' she yelps, continuing to batter me with the ex-Chihuahua.

When the whacking stops, I peep out. 'Sorry, Treacle.'

She's pacing again. 'I'm hopeless. I'm going to mess it up, I know I will!'

'No you won't.' I leap up. 'You'll be great, and Mrs Simpson will be nice, and you'll get on really well.' I'm keeping pace with her, backward and forward, hopping over the clothes and books littering my floor.

Treacle sinks on to the bed and drops her head into her hands. 'Why do I have to meet Jeff's parents at all?'

'I guess he's planning to date you for a while,' I say with a smile.

Treacle groans and flops back on to the crumpled duvet. 'Yeah well, he might change his mind after I've told his mother she's a stupid old bag.'

'You won't.' I plop down beside her and pass her a sandwich. 'He won't. It'll be fine.'

Treacle sits up and takes a bite, staring despairingly into space as she chews. 'Perhaps Jessica Jupiter can write something in Jeff's horoscope this week asking him to be sympathetic and understanding if a loved one happens to say something dumb.'

'Good idea,' I agree. 'Just in case.' Jessica Jupiter's my alter-ego – I write horoscopes for the school webzine under her name. It's the silliest job on the webzine and far less cool than Will Bold's job as feature writer, or Jeff's role as sports writer. Even boring Barbara Tweed has a better job than me, with her brainless lifestyle features. (Most earth-shattering articles to date: *Twenty Ways to Get the Most from Your School Locker, Desk Etiquette: Polite Behaviour in the Classroom* and *Top Tips to Spice Up Your School Stationery*.) At least no one apart from Treacle knows I'm Jessica Jupiter. I'd die of embarrassment. I joined the webzine team as the first step on the ladder of my career in journalism. It was going to be the line on my CV that landed me my first intern job on the local paper; the local paper was going to lead to a national paper, and within five years I was going to be writing my own column and winning international awards. My head fills with my favourite fantasy – a wide stage stretching around me, an audience glittering in the darkness as I stand at the podium, accepting the award for Journalist of the Year.

Treacle nudges me and passes me a glass of milk. 'Thank goodness we've got Jessica on our side.' She takes a creamy sip from her glass, then licks away her milk moustache. 'If it wasn't for her, Jeff might never have noticed my number ten shirt.'

'Jessica' had written in Jeff's horoscope that the

number ten would change his life. When he spotted it on Treacle's football jersey after she'd scored the winning goal at the Year Nine girls' football cup final, he asked her out. It was a major result for Jessica, and I was delighted to help my best friend land the boy of her dreams.

I start thinking about this week's column. I've written most of it already. But I left Cancer and Pisces till last. Jeff's star sign is Cancer – and I know what to write now, but Pisces will be harder. 'I'm stuck on Savannah's sign,' I tell Treacle.

'Pisces?'

'I want to use this week's prediction to warn her.'

'About LJ?'

I nod and we both sip at our milk.

'Do you think I should interfere?' I ask. 'What if we're wrong about LJ?'

'Were we wrong about Josh?' Treacle reminds me.

'No,' I concede. Josh was Savannah's last boyfriend and, when I spotted him snogging Chelsea Leeson behind the bike shed, I'd used Jessica's column to warn Savannah that he couldn't be trusted.

'You don't have to be totally down on LJ,' Treacle suggests. 'Maybe just hint that the new boy may need to *earn* his reputation as coolest kid in school.'

LJ is a Year Ten who has just moved to Green Park High from a school in America. Everyone treats him like a god and he laps it up, never missing a chance to remind them that he was a model in the US – glossing over the less-than-glamorous fact that most of his work has been for catalogues, and an advert for pet food. Watching him strut around the school corridors you'd think he'd spent the past three years on a New York catwalk. And he checks himself in every door or window that reflects his glorious passing. 'Bleugh!' I pull a face, wondering what on earth Savannah sees in him. He's good-looking, but he knows it. 'Why can't she go out with Marcus? He's had a crush on her for ages and he's really sweet.'

'Savannah's determined to land a Year Ten.' Treacle shrugs.

I slide her a sideways glance. 'It's pretty rare for a Year Nine to date a Year Ten.'

She grins, clearly thinking of Jeff. 'I did manage to shrug off the Year Nine Invisibility Cloak, didn't I?'

'You've brought hope to us all,' I tell her. Year Nine sucks. You're not in the top year, not in the bottom. Not doing GCSEs, not allowed to work in the tuck shop. Year Tens are usually blind to Year Nines. I know this better than most – all the other kids on the webzine are Year Tens and most of the time they treat me like I'm not there. If they do notice me, it's to give me any idiot job that happens to be available. And Cindy – our editor and the school's resident Ice Queen – is the only one who knows I'm the webzine's star-sign scribbler because she gave me the dumb job in the first place.

The only webziner who treats me like I can actually read and write is Sam Baynham, the music reporter. He even invited me out for a milkshake once, but I think that was just because he felt sorry for me because Ben had been ill. I said no, of course. I'm no pity case, and I wanted to catch the bus to the hospital and visit Ben.

Treacle drains her glass noisily, jerking me from my thoughts.

'So what are you going to write for Savannah? Sorry. What's *Jessica* going to write?' she corrects herself. 'Is she going to set Sav straight about LJ?'

'She'll try,' I promise. The thought of writing horoscopes for the rest of the term makes my stomach tighten. 'But I don't think I'll be able to help people with the horoscopes for much longer.'

Treacle raises her eyebrows. 'Why?'

'Because I have a plan,' I say, reaching for another sandwich. 'A plan to remove Jessica Jupiter from my life once and for all.'

The form room is cosy after the freezing dash from the bus stop. I can still feel the sting of the biting March wind on my cheeks. Ryan Edwards is breathing steam on to a window and doodling faces. Chelsea is perched on a radiator, her skinny legs hooked on to a desk. Josh slouches beside her, his arm round her shoulders, like a snake hanging off a stick.

'Hey, Chelsea!' Anila calls across the room. 'Don't burn your bum.'

Chelsea sticks out her tongue and snuggles closer to Josh.

I nudge Treacle, swivelling my eyeballs toward Savannah, and whisper, 'Do Josh and Chelsea have to smooch in front of everyone?' But Savannah's not flinging vengeful looks at the love-rats today. She's leaning swoonily against the wall beside Treacle, hugging her backpack and gazing into space.

'LJ's wearing bow-legged jeans,' she sighs. 'Only a real model could carry off a pair of low-waisters like that. He's so *gorgeous*.' She fixes me with an intense stare.

'Did I tell you he used to drive his Dad's Cadillac to school when he lived in America? He's so far ahead of anyone here. He must think Green Park is *so* totally backward.'

Treacle's eyebrows lift, 'Yeah, right.'

Miss Davis scuttles into the room and opens the class register. 'Hello, everyone.' She beams like a lighthouse. 'Nasty weather today.'

Savannah stares dreamily out of the window. 'I hadn't noticed,' she sighs.

I hate to diss Savannah. She's a babe and really sweet with it. If there's a trend, she's setting it; there's no outfit she can't wear and her porcelain skin has never hosted a spot. She's kind, thoughtful and friends with everyone – and me and Treacle are lucky to have her as a best friend. *But* she suffers from boy-blindness. Sav gets so dazzled by good looks she can't tell heroes from zeroes. She should date blindfolded.

'Don't you know he's in *so* love with himself, he'll never notice you?' Treacle tells Savannah bluntly.

Miss Davis starts calling names from the register. 'Tracy Brown.'

Treacle shoots up her hand, 'Here.'

Savannah sniffs and takes a compact from her bag. 'Just because he's cool and good-looking, doesn't mean he's not a nice guy.' She ducks to get a glimpse of herself while she dabs her perfect nose with powder. 'I don't see

17

why you're so cynical, Treacle. You landed Jeff,' she snaps her compact shut, 'Dreams *do* come true.'

'Jeff's a nice guy,' I point out.

Savannah tips her head. 'And what makes you think LJ's not?'

OK, she's got a point. I've got no proof. I'm going on gut instinct. Every time I see LJ, he's surrounded by a crowd and looking like he's wishing he could give autographs. But gut instinct is not enough. A real journalist needs facts. If only there was some way I could get evidence that he's as shallow as a puddle.

A headline pops into my mind:

School Glamour-boy Exposed!

Green Park new boy, LJ, revealed in an in-depth interview with reporter Gemma Stone that he actually didn't know the name of a single one of his classmates.

'Gee. It never occurred to me that British people had actual given names,' he admitted. 'I've just been calling them whatever popped into my head. No one seemed to mind so I thought I must be the only person in school with a proper name.'

'Gemma Stone?' Miss Davis's voice zaps my thoughts. She's looking up from her desk. 'Gemma?' She scans the room.

I stick up my hand. 'Here!'

'Anila Zajmi.' Miss Davis finishes the register just as the bell goes for first lesson.

Savannah's off like a whippet. 'Come on.' She hooks her arm through Treacle's and drags her away.

'Wait for me!' I follow them to the crush at the door.

We pass Marcus and I can't help noticing his wistful gaze follow Savannah. Marcus asked her out last month, but she chose Josh and hasn't looked at Marcus since, even though he's ten times sweeter than Josh and cute in his own shy way.

We burst out of the form room and into the hallway.

Treacle's flapping from Savannah's arm like washing on a windy day. 'What's the hurry?' I ask.

'We're going the long way,' Savannah announces. Instead of turning right towards the classroom where Mrs Dalton is thumping English Literature books on to desks in readiness for our arrival, she veers left and scoots along the corridor towards the science labs.

Treacle gives me the desperate stare of a kidnap victim as I catch up.

'Are you trying to shed calories?' I ask Savannah, mystified why she should circle the entire building to get to the classroom just next door to our form room.

'Never miss a chance to exercise,' Savannah puffs, swinging Treacle round the corner as the corridor splits. We hit a wave of students and weave through the surge like salmon fighting their way upstream. As we round the next corner, I understand why Savannah's taking the long route. LJ is at the far end of the hallway, leaning next to the science-lab door.

'Savannah!' The sigh in Treacle's voice is enough to tell me she's spotted LJ too.

He's watching his classmates file into the lesson – or rather, he's letting *them* watch *him*. Each girl drifts past, glancing up hopefully. LJ's gaze flicks over them like a farmer inspecting cattle. He doesn't crack a smile.

I suddenly realize Savannah's disappeared towards LJ. 'Quick, let's rescue her before she does something stupid,' I gasp to Treacle, who rolls her eyes.

'Gem, if you're worried she's going to throw herself at LJ, she'll have to join the queue.'

But the queue's quickly dwindling as LJ's classmates disappear into the lab.

'Come on!' I grab Treacle's arm and drag her forwards. Savannah's smoothing her long blonde hair with her hand and gazing at LJ.

I tap her shoulder. 'We're going to be late for English.'

'One more minute,' Savannah pleads. 'The bell's only just gone.'

I glance back along the corridor. It's become ominously empty and quiet.

'He's not even noticed you,' Treacle tries to reason with Savannah.

LJ's stare is fixed on a window, where he's staring at his reflection in the glass. He lifts a hand to re-tousle the thick, brown hair flopping over his eyes.

'Let's go, Sav—' I stop as Sam looms in front of me.

'Hi, Gemma.' His bright blue eyes meet mine and he does one of his I'm-totally-unaware-how-gorgeous-I-am smiles. If only LJ were more like Sam, Savannah might be in with a chance.

'Hi, Sam.' I nod toward the science lab. 'Is this your class?'

'Double Physics,' he shrugs. 'Not a bad way to start a Monday.'

I'm surprised to discover he's a science-head. 'I thought you were only into music.'

Sam grins. 'Yeah, well, I like to stay in tune with the whole universe.'

Behind me I hear Savannah giggle and my heart sinks. It's her flirty giggle. I turn round and find her simpering at LJ.

'Hi, LJ. How's it going?' she asks.

Treacle pulls a face at me, sticking out her tongue like she's about to heave.

LJ looks down at Savannah. 'Oh – er – hi …' He frowns like he's fumbling for a long-forgotten memory. 'I know you, right?' His American accent sounds more American than the ones on TV. 'You're – er – Tundra, aren't you?'

21

Sam jabs him in the arm. 'She's *Savannah*, you idiot.'

LJ scratches the side of his nose. 'I knew it was some kinda climate zone.' He turns and disappears into the lab.

Savannah watches him go like a leper who has just been blessed by the Pope.

Sam shakes his head. 'That new kid is not the brightest tool in the box.'

'"Tool" is right,' Treacle mutters beside me.

I elbow her sharply, hoping Sam didn't hear, but he's looking at Treacle, eyes narrow. 'I thought every girl in Green Park was in the LJ fan club.'

Treacle wrinkles her nose. 'He calls football "soccer" and thinks it was invented by Americans,' she huffs.

Sam's eyes twinkle beneath his shaggy blond hair. 'Maybe he's still jet-lagged. Hopefully he'll catch up soon.' His gaze flicks back to me. 'Are you coming to the webzine HQ at lunchtime?'

I nod. 'I want to start work on my—' I stop myself just in time. I can't say 'horoscopes'. No one apart from Cindy and Treacle know that I'm Jessica Jupiter. I grope for words. 'My – er – the – er – lipstick review I'm doing for Cindy.'

Cindy keeps giving me make-up to test for her beauty column. It's her way of disguising my role as horoscope writer. She calls me the webzine's editorial assistant, but

22

basically I'm a lab rat. I keep expecting animal rights activists to break in and release me back into the wild.

'What are you testing this week?' Sam asks.

'Fang-Bang Ruby Lip-Shimmer.' I cringe, wanting to explain that I joined the webzine to be a reporter, not a guinea pig for beauty products.

Sam throws out a hand to catch the fast-closing door of the science lab. 'Some girls don't need make-up,' he says as he slides through the gap and disappears into his lesson.

He must be talking about Cindy. Her face is more painted than the Mona Lisa's, but I think she'd be far prettier without make-up. She has blue eyes, rosebud lips and cheekbones you could slice cheese with.

'Did you hear him?' Savannah's hanging off my arm, staring at the lab door. 'He actually *spoke* to me.'

I look at her, surprised. 'Who?'

Savannah looks at me, round-eyed. 'LJ, of course! Didn't you hear him?'

Treacle puffs out her cheeks. 'He called you "Tundra".'

'So?' Savannah heads down the corridor. 'Did you see the way he looked at me, Gem?'

A wave of despair crashes over me as I follow her. She's besotted. 'He looked like he was trying to remember who you were,' I remind her.

'Exactly!' Savannah pauses at the English-room door. 'And he *did* remember me.'

'A girl called "Tundra"'s hard to forget,' Treacle mutters.

'"Tundra"'s almost the same as "Savannah",' Savannah argues.

Treacle reaches for the door handle. 'Try telling that to a penguin.'

I can see Mrs Dalton through the meshed glass of the door window. She's pacing the front of the class, book in hand. Ryan's head is resting on his desk and Sally Moore is mouthing something to Anila. The lesson is clearly in full swing. 'Come on!' I nudge Treacle.

'Wait.' Savannah pulls a pot of strawberry lipbalm from her blazer pocket. 'This weather is murder on my lips.' As she flicks off the lid, her mouth drops open. 'Look!' She thrusts the balm under my nose.

I stare at it. 'What?'

'Can't you see it?' Savannah sounds amazed.

Treacle leans over the pot and stares. 'What?'

'It spells LJ!' Savannah proclaims.

'What does?' Treacle sounds unconvinced.

'The marks in the lipbalm.' She points at a couple of smears in the pink goo. 'It definitely says LJ!'

I squint, trying to make out a pattern. 'It's just squiggles,' I say.

Savannah snatches the pot away. 'It's not just squiggles! It's a sign! It clearly says LJ! I knew we were meant to be together!'

The door of the English room swings open. Mrs Dalton frowns at us over her half-specs. 'Very good of you to join us,' she says sarcastically.

'Sorry, Miss.' I duck past her and slide into my seat. As Treacle sits beside me, Savannah floats to the back of the class, her eyes dreamy.

I can't believe LJ has reduced Savannah to such a twittering idiot. I pull my books from my bag, vowing to take immediate action to end her insanity.

I'm writing Savannah's horoscope in my head as I take the stairs to the webzine HQ. There's only twenty minutes to the bell for the first lesson after lunch. Escaping the lunch room took longer than I'd planned; Savannah was using me as a human shield while she watched LJ pick his way through a box of sushi.

He used chopsticks.

She practically fell off her chair with excitement. 'Oh. My. God! He is *so cool!*'

Substitute 'lame' for 'cool' and she pretty much got it right.

I glance at my watch – nineteen minutes left – and open the door.

The webzine HQ is basically a storeroom on the first floor of the school. The caretaker kindly cleared out most of the clutter and now, apart from the shelves of aging textbooks and glue pots that line the walls, there are six battered desks, each with a computer and a chair.

No one's here. I've got the room to myself. I wonder

where they are. It's deadline day. I can't be the only one who's not finished their piece. Maybe the rest of the webzine team have already been and gone. Maybe amazement at LJ's chopstick skills slayed them and they're lying dead in a corridor somewhere, their faces frozen in awe.

The ticker tape starts running in my head.

Newsroom Massacre

The entire staff of the Green Park High webzine were struck down today, stunned to death by the unprece-dented coolness of their new schoolmate.

LJ Kennedy, recently arrived from the USA, ate sushi in the lunch room with chopsticks. In a community where forks and fingers rule the lunch box, this startling feat of manual dexterity plunged the entire school into hysteria.

Webzine editor, Cindy Jensen, was the first to suc-cumb, frothing at the mouth as shock overwhelmed her. Will Bold collapsed a few minutes later, his face con-torted as he landed on his editor's still-writhing body, though it's not yet clear whether it was astonishment or contempt that killed him.

The old school clock above the door is ticking away the seconds noisily. I cut the internal monologue.

I breathe in the lovely old paper-and-wood smell of

the storeroom as I settle behind a desk. It's how I imagine a newsroom might have smelled in the days before plastic and high-speed communication. I've bagged the fastest PC, pleased that Will's not here to elbow his way to it like he usually does. By the time I've got the PC humming, found this week's horoscope document and opened it, Savannah's stars are already written in my head. It takes me two seconds to slip into Jessica Jupiter's voice and type them into the PC.

Pisces. You are the most idealistic and dreamy of all the star signs, but don't be fish-brained, Star-ling. Before you dive into a new romance, check the depth. You may think you've found your heart's desire but, my dear Fin-derella, your Prince Charming may turn out to be all charm and no prince.

I pause, leaning back in my chair. It may not be enough to convince Savannah. I know from experience that when she's smitten, the smit runs deep. Frowning, I tap my fingernails on the desk – I gave up biting my nails when I became Jessica. Somehow, chewed stubs for fingers didn't suit the glamorous image I'd given her. Though I still have to fight the urge to nibble. Then an idea strikes. I could encourage Marcus to ask Savannah out again. It might distract her. After all, a real date beats a fantasy date. I've actually only ever had fantasy dates, so I don't know for sure, but it seems logical. I can do a quick search on Facebook to find out Marcus's birthday – then I can work out his star sign and lace his horoscope with gentle encouragement to try again.

As I log in to the website, the storeroom door swings open.

'Hi.' It's Sam.

I half look up from my keyboard as I type Marcus's name into the search box. 'Hi.'

'Have you heard the news?' He sounds excited.

'What news?' I ask, looking up properly now.

Sam's perched on the desk opposite, staring at me with eager puppy eyes. 'About my band.'

'Your band?' I hit the return key to enter my search.

'We've been given a regular slot playing at the under-age night at Sounds on Fridays.'

'Wow!' No wonder he looks so happy. Sounds is a nightclub in town. It's normally eighteen-and-over but a couple of weeks ago they announced that there was going to be an underage night the first Friday of every month – so anyone from fourteen to eighteen can go. And this month every Friday night before midnight is teens only, as a kind of promotional thing, so getting a regular gig there is very cool. 'That's brilliant! I guess your new set is working.'

'Yeah.' His fingers fidget on the edge of the desk. 'It's sounding pretty good.' He's hiding behind his shaggy blond fringe. It's cute that he's self-conscious about his own music when he's so passionate about other bands.

'I'm really pleased for you,' I tell him sincerely. 'You deserve it.'

'Thanks.'

I glance back at my screen, expecting to see a neat list of Marcus Bainbridges. But there's no sign of search results; just my profile. And headlining my profile are the words: 'Marcus Bainbridge'.

What?

Horror creeps over me like cold, dead fingers.

No!

I've typed Marcus's name into my *status* box, not the search box.

Quick! Change it!

As I grab for the mouse, Cindy swings in. 'I want a quick word with everyone before the bell goes,' she announces briskly.

Will blows in after her. 'Thanks, Gemma.' He leans across my desk, steals the mouse from my fingers and clicks my browser window shut. 'You've saved me having to wait for it to start up.'

'B-but—' I stare at him, open mouthed.

'Sorry.' He's nudging me out of my chair. 'But you can play on Facebook in the IT suite. I've got *real* work to do.'

I get to my feet, giving him angry eyes.

'What?' He looks at me in bewilderment. 'You *know* this is my PC.'

Sam straightens. 'They belong to everyone, Will.'

Will shrugs towards the computer on the next desk. 'Then she can use that one.'

Cindy butts in. 'Look, guys,' she says, using her reasoning-with-toddlers voice, 'it's deadline day and I've had no submissions. I want them finished before this afternoon's deadline meeting. It's a big job, you know, checking them all over before they go out on Wednesday morning.'

I'm hardly listening to the Ice Queen's pity-plea. I'm staring in dismay at Will's PC. I've just published Marcus as my status! Everyone's going to think I'm obsessed with him.

'Gemma?' Cindy taps her foot.

'Yeah?' I dive for the computer on the next desk and switch it on. Two minutes to the bell. *Come on!*

'I hope you've got some feedback for me on the lip-shimmer.'

Will's eyes light up. 'Haven't you finished your piece either, Cinders?'

'I'm waiting for Gemma's input.' I guess Cindy wants to find out if I've finished the horoscopes but, right now, I don't care. I'm too busy willing the PC to hurry up.

'Can't you write the reviews yourself?' Will asks innocently. 'I thought if you had a valid opinion on *anything*, it'd be make up.'

My fury doubles. Why steal my PC, then spend the

last two minutes of break teasing Cindy? The school login screen appears and I type in my username. As the hard drive whirs and clicks, the lesson bell starts wailing.

No!

'I'll see you at the meeting.' Sam's leaving. I don't look up. My eyes are fixed on my screen. The task bar's hardly appeared.

Hurry up!

Will shuts down his PC and heads for the door.

Cindy evil-eyes him as he passes, then looks at me. 'Come on.'

'I'll only be a minute,' I snap.

I sense her prickle. '*Now!*' She marches past my desk and switches the power off at the wall.

The screen turns black in front of me.

'Why did you do that?' I ask through clenched teeth.

'If the webzine starts making us late for lessons, they'll close us down.'

I breathe deeply. The Ice Queen has just destroyed my life *again* but I'm not going to give her the satisfaction of seeing me upset. Instead I grab my bag and slide past her, replaying her death by LJ's chopsticks in my head.

I stomp to Maths, blind with rage and despair. Now I won't be able to change my Facebook status till school ends. What if someone sees it? Oh, God, I'll die!

Shoulders drooping, head down to hide the tears of frustration pricking at my eyes, I join the swarm streaming into the Maths room. Treacle's already there. I slide into the seat next to her, flushed.

'What's up?' Treacle asks as chairs scrape and clatter around us.

'I've messed up my Facebook status,' I whimper. 'I was searching for Marcus to find his star sign and I put him in my status box instead of the search box.'

Treacle moves in closer. 'But you deleted it, right?'

'No!' I wail. 'Cindy came in and started burbling on and Will pushed me off the computer and then the bell went.' Frustration is boiling in my stomach.

Treacle bites her lip. 'You can change it after school before anyone sees it,' she says encouragingly.

'Yeah.' I feel a glimmer of hope. I'm not the only one stuck in lessons. Surely, no one's going to check Facebook before they get home from school.

My ray of hope shines for about three seconds. Then Treacle nudges me.

She's staring at Ryan and Marcus, two desks ahead. From here I can see Ryan's smartphone under the desk. Its blue glow is lighting up Marcus's leg. Marcus is peering down, squinting.

My heart drops like a stone as I recognize the blue and white of the Facebook site. Ryan is showing off his page. As he tilts his phone closer to Marcus, he glances over his shoulder at me. His eyes are bright with amusement.

'Oh. My. God. He's seen it!' I hiss at Treacle.

Marcus turns in his seat. I glimpse his amazed expression before I drop my head and bury my gaze in my maths books. My cheeks have caught fire. He's going to think I'm crazy about him.

Time slows. The Double Maths lesson drags through the afternoon like walking through porridge. At last, the bell signals the end of the day.

I spring from my seat and hare for the door.

'I'll phone you later,' Treacle calls.

'Yeah!' I'm out the door, across the hall and hopping up the stairs to the webzine HQ three at a time. An Olympic champion couldn't have made the distance faster.

When I burst into the storeroom, I'm horrified to see all six PCs occupied. Cindy, Will, Jeff, Sam, Barbara, Dave and Phil are all here.

'How did you get here so fast?' I gasp.

Barbara looks up. 'Hi, Gemma.' She smiles. 'Year Ten study period. We're finishing our pieces before the deadline meeting.'

Cindy's tapping away on the PC closest to the window. 'Which starts in two minutes.'

Will's hammering his keyboard. 'Make it five,' he comments without pausing. 'Need to finish this paragraph.'

Jeff's got his head down, frowning as he types.

'Jeff,' I ask tentatively, 'can I borrow your PC, just for a minute?'

He shakes his head. 'Sorry, Gem, just finishing this match report. I won't be long.'

Will shifts in his seat. 'Can't you wait till you get home to check Facebook?'

I fight the urge to hurl my schoolbag at him. 'There's something important I *have* to do!'

'How important can it be?' he snaps back. 'You're just the assistant.'

His words stick me like a stiletto. *You just wait, Will Bold! I'm going to grab the first chance I get and show you what I can do!*

'Do you want to use this one?' Sam gets up from his seat.

Gratitude floods me. 'Thanks, Sam, you're a life-saver.'

Cindy clears her throat. 'I hope everyone's finished.'

Will gives his keyboard a final battering and then leans back in his chair looking pleased with himself. 'I'm done.'

No!

'Let's get started then.' Cindy hoists her chair over her desk and parks it in front. With a clatter, the rest of the team copy her, circling their chairs round the middle of the room.

'Can I just make a quick change . . .?' I stare longingly at Sam's PC.

Cindy freezes me with an arctic look. 'Some of us have

buses to catch. Do you want to make *everyone* late, Gemma?'

Everyone is looking at me expectantly.

'No,' I sigh.

'Well, grab a chair and sit down,' Cindy orders.

My heart is as heavy as lead. I haul a chair over Sam's desk and plonk it beside Dave's.

As my universe collapses around me, Cindy reaches for her clipboard. 'Item number one.'

Oh, God. This meeting is going to take forever.

The whole world will have time to get home, eat a snack, see my Facebook status and start a comment-fest I don't even want to imagine.

'Right.' Cindy taps her pen on her clipboard. 'Now on to article submissions. Has everyone finished their piece for this week?'

A nod goes round the circle like a Mexican wave.

'Good.' She makes a tick on her agenda. 'What have we got?' She scans the group, her blonde bob flicking against her cheeks. 'Dave?'

Dave Senior pushes his glasses up his nose. 'Phil and I have been reviewing the latest *Space Cops* shoot-em-up,' he announces.

Sam grins. 'I've tried it too,' he confesses. 'It's fantastic. Great range of weapons.'

Phil's nodding. 'The game-play's good too. Nice, tight plotting. Good learning curve. You don't end up dead on the first mission, but the third one is challenging enough to keep you playing.'

Barbara blinks at him with the earnestness of a middle-aged owl. 'Doesn't the violence worry you?'

Phil looks at her like she's just asked him if he's scared of monsters. 'Why should it? It's not real.'

Sam leans forward in his chair. 'Did you see the trap on level two?'

Dave slaps his knee. 'I fell into it four times before I came up with a workaround.'

Phil's nodding now. 'You have to shoot the compound guard *before* you enter the walkway.'

Cindy rolls her eyes. 'Yes, yes. We get the picture.' Her gaze shoots back to Dave. 'How many words did you write?'

'Six hundred and fifty-two.'

'Good.' Cindy makes a sharp tick on her agenda. 'Now, Jeff, which matches have you covered this week?'

Jeff leans back in his chair, tipping it on to its hind legs. 'The rugby under fifteens and the Senior Swimming Gala. And I've listed the results of the Year Nine netball playoffs.'

'Great.' Cindy makes another tick on her clipboard, then turns to Barbara. 'I hope you've got another of your wonderful lifestyle articles for us, Barbie.'

Frustration flares in my chest. Barbara's pieces to date have been so dull I've had to break off reading to stick forks in my eyes for light relief. One of them was called *Homework Presentation – Twelve Steps to Neatness* for goodness' sake. I could do *so* much better. There are three ideas jostling in my head right now: *Eating Disorders: the Five Warning Signs*, *Get a Head Start on Your Dream Job: Ten Aspirational Tips* and *Year Tens: one thousand and one Reasons Why They Should be Home-schooled'*.

I'm grinding my teeth. Barbara only got the job as lifestyle features writer because she's Cindy's best friend. The two of them have been inseparable since nursery school, even though Cindy looks like she fell off the cover of *Vogue* and Barbara looks like she fell out of a recycling bin. I can picture them now, sitting in Cindy's perfectly pink bedroom, toasting marshmallows over a candle while they share their innermost secrets.

'Oh, Barbie,' Cindy turns her mallow as it blisters over the tiny flame. 'It would be *ab-fab* if you'd write the dullest thing you can think of this week.'

'Oh, Cindy,' Barbara simpers back, 'I have a perfect idea.'

Cindy's hand flutters to her throat excitedly. 'Is it duller than your piece on homework? I'm hoping to actually bore a reader to *death* this week.'

'Well, this piece will do it.' Barbara nods eagerly. 'It's far duller than anything I've written so far.'

My rose-coloured fantasy fades as real-life Barbara tugs her shapeless brown skirt to cover her knees. I notice the wrinkles in her thick fawn tights and wonder if she'd like the tweed suit I bought for Treacle.

'This week I've moved the focus to relationships,' she announces proudly.

I sit up. Could she possibly have written something

interesting? *Ten Kissing Secrets You Don't Know; The First Date: How Far Should You Go?*

Barbara gives a wide smile. *Why Teachers Are Our Friends.*

This girl is from Planet Dweeb! I'm not surprised when Will laughs out loud.

Cindy hurls him a glare.

I search the expressions of the rest of the team. Sam's scratching his head. 'How can teachers be our friends?'

Barbara leans forward, concern clouding her round brown eyes. 'How can they *not* be?' she breathes earnestly. 'They do so much for us – I really don't think we appreciate that. If we did, we could get so much more from them and from our education.'

Will leans forward to meet her eye. 'Are you serious?'

'Absolutely.' Barbara's gaze doesn't waver. She might not be the coolest chick in Green Park High, but I admire the way she makes no apology for what she thinks or feels.

Will leans back with a shrug. 'Whatever.'

'Barbara, that sounds really great. I'm looking forward to reading it.' Cindy makes a note on her clipboard then she turns to Will. 'What have you got for us this week?'

Will slowly crosses his legs. 'Solid, fact-based prose as usual,' he drawls. 'I don't want to bore you with the details.'

Cindy's lips twitch. Drawing her perfectly plucked brows into a sympathetic frown, she reaches out and touches his knee. 'Don't worry, Will.' Her voice is like syrup. 'If it's boring I can always brighten it up here and there when I edit.'

He swipes her hand away. 'Don't you dare!' he snarls. 'I don't want it ruined by your frilly prose.'

'Calm down, William.' Cindy leans back, a slow smile on her lips. 'Go on then, tell us what it's about. We're all *dying* to know.'

He fries her with a death stare. 'Revision,' he growls.

'Ooh.' Barbara claps her hands together. 'How helpful. Do you give tips on how to revise more effectively?'

Will doesn't even look at her. He's still barbequing Cindy with flame-eyes but he can't shift her smug grin. 'It's about the dangers of *over*-revising,' he says. 'I've quoted medical reports, specialist opinion and given case studies.'

'Sounds fascinating.' Cindy makes a leisurely tick on her clipboard. 'I can hardly wait to read it.'

Will sits up, his face dark with menace. 'What's *your* piece about, Cinders?'

Cindy raises her chin. We're glued to our seats like monkeys watching the gorillas fight.

'I've written an *amazing* article on how certain foods are linked to ugliness.'

How certain foods are linked to ugliness! Where does she get this nonsense? Will's going to annihilate her.

He slides down in his chair and grins. 'I knew you could eat yourself thin, but I didn't know you could eat yourself pretty.'

'Oh, yes.' Cindy's earnest now. 'It's totally up to us whether we're pretty of not. A good diet is key to good looks. Too many carbs make you sallow and jowly, while raw vegetables will give you the face and figure of a supermodel.'

I shrink behind my frothing curls. She must think I eat nothing but crusts.

Will folds his arms. 'Perhaps you could give a PowerPoint presentation to the canteen staff,' he suggests. 'Green Park could do with a few supermodels.'

I scowl at him. Is that what it takes to get liked by him? Supermodel looks? If I ever have a boyfriend, he's going to love me for my mind.

Who am I kidding? I slump in my seat. It would be fantastic if boys thought I was stunning, despite my wildly curly hair and freckly nose.

'It's getting late.' Sam glances at the clock. 'Shall I tell you about my piece, then we can call it a day?'

Cindy tucks her hair behind one ear. 'I was saving you till last, Sam,' she says in her honey voice.

Sam rubs his palms on his knees. 'I checked out a new band, the Raging Dwarves.'

Cindy sucks the end of her pen. 'Cool.'

'Great live band,' he says. 'Good atmosphere. And I made a list of this week's top-ten MP3 downloads. Added a few comments.' He runs his fingers through his hair. 'Just my opinion. Everyone's taste is different.'

'Sounds great, Sam.' Cindy's too busy winding her pen round a stray tendril of silky hair to make a tick on her clipboard. 'I'm sure our readers will love it.'

Will grunts. 'Sounds a lot better than your eat-fruit-look-cute piece.'

Cindy rounds on him, turning from gentle lamb to big bad wolf in a blink. 'At least I don't bore my readers using statistics to state the obvious. What are you working on next week, Will? A well-researched piece that proves *some* boys are taller than *some* girls?'

Will rubs his nose. 'Next week's piece will blow you away, Cinders.'

'Really, Will?' Cindy narrows her eyes. 'Why don't you tell us about it?'

'It's secret.'

'Is that because it doesn't exist?'

'Yes, it does.'

'Prove it.'

'I don't have to prove anything to you.'

I sit up. My brain is whirring, this growling match could be the perfect opportunity to get myself upgraded from horoscopes. I give Will my best doe-eyed look. 'Perhaps it's something I can help you with?'

He looks at me like I'm a monkey who just learned to talk. '*You?*'

It's just the reaction I'd hoped for. I look appealingly at Cindy, pleased to see her eyes flash. I knew it, she's not going to miss this chance to sabotage Will.

'What a splendid idea, Gemma.'

She's taken the bait. I hold on to my chair, swallowing back excitement. The deal's not sealed yet.

Will's staring at me. 'How can *she* help *me?*'

I stare back, my smile fixed.

'She's our editorial assistant,' Cindy reminds him. 'Helping out is what she's here for.'

I brace myself for Will's reply when the door opens and Mr Harris peers round. 'Oh good,' he says happily. 'You're still here. Just thought I'd check in to see how it's all going. Are we on track for the next edition?'

'Cinderella over there wants me to let a Year Nine help out with my next article,' Will complains.

Cindy looks up at Mr Harris warmly. 'It'll be such good experience for Gemma,' she gushes. 'I know she's been dying for a chance to get involved in a more serious way.'

Mr Harris nods approvingly. 'What a great idea.' He smiles at me. 'Are you up for it, Gemma?'

'Oh, yes!' I know I'm just a banana Cindy's hurling at

Will, but I don't care. If it lands me a real assignment, it's worth it.

'OK, then.' Mr Harris turns to Will. 'I'm sure you'll find Gemma a great asset.'

Will's knuckles are white as he clutches the edges of his chair. 'OK, Mr Harris,' he mutters through clenched teeth.

'Good, good.' Mr Harris glances round the room. 'Well it seems like you have everything under control, Cindy. Anything else I can help with?' he asks distract-edly.

'No, thank you, Mr Harris.' Cindy's nice as pie.

'Good, good.' Mr Harris withdraws, shutting the door. I thank whichever god sent him.

'Excellent.' Cindy snaps the agenda off her clipboard. 'I think that's enough for today.'

I half expect Will to lunge forward and throttle her but he just grabs his bag and stomps out.

As the rest of the team start shrugging on their jack-ets and grabbing their bags, I freeze in my seat. My stomach feels suddenly hollow.

What have I done? I'm helping Will on a serious article!

The dark shadow of failure looms over me like a threatening storm. What if I mess it up and prove that I'm not good enough for anything but horoscopes?

'Get down!' Will's hiss echoes round the darkened ware-house.

I duck down beside him, sheltering behind a row of metal barrels. Peering through the midnight gloom, I can just make out a van.

Two burly men are pushing a group of huddled men and women into the back.

'These are the vans that drive them to mushroom caves,' Will whispers.

'And this happens *every* night?' I take my reporter's notebook from my pocket.

It's an imaginary notebook of course. In the real world. I'm dunking spag-bol-stained plates into washing-up water. But, in my head, I'm helping Will expose a dangerous gang of human traffickers.

'Every night.' Will slides a mini video cam out of his pocket. 'I've been staking this place out for a week. It's the same story. Those men herd the immigrants on to a bus, drive them to the mushroom caves for a night's harvesting, then bring them back at dawn.'

I grab a saucepan and plunge it into the warm soapy water. Gloopy pasta is stuck on the bottom. As I attack it with my scrubber, a loud clang booms through the shadowy warehouse. The men have slammed the van doors shut. They swing up into the cab and rev the engine. Petrol fumes sting my nose.

I scrub at the sticky rim of the pan, then hold it under the cold tap, watching the bubbles rinse down the plug-hole.

Wheels screech on wet concrete and the van hares out of the half-opened door at the far end.

'Come on.' Will ducks out from behind the barrels. 'We don't have much time.'

I gaze in the washing-up bowl, glazing over as I watch rainbow pools of grease float past fast-dying bubbles.

Water's dripping from the rafters high above our heads. I hurry after Will, heart hammering, as we run the length of the warehouse, splashing through oily puddles.

'In here.' Will zigzags between steel pillars to a wire mesh staircase, then starts to climb, his footsteps clanging on the metal steps.

I follow, breathless by the time we reach the top and head along a walkway high above the ground.

I grope for cutlery at the bottom of the washing-up bowl. As I poke at spaghetti, gunked between the fork prongs, Will edges toward a steel-clad room built in among the rafters.

He pauses at the metal door. 'I can't hear anyone.'

I take a torch from my pocket and hand it to him. 'You might need this.'

'Good thinking, Gem,' he whispers and steps across the threshold.

I reach behind me for the frying pan that's still on the hob, and dunk it into the water.

Will flicks on my torch. Its beam lights up the floor, highlighting a jumble of sleeping bags, clothes and blankets.

I gasp. 'How many people sleep in here?'

Will shrugs. 'Between twenty and thirty.'

The air is thick and hot, and the smell of stale sweat makes me feel sick.

'Give me the torch,' I tell Will. 'Then you can video.'

Will starts to tape what we're seeing. I can't wait to publish this.

'Over there.' He nods toward a corner, to a stinking bucket.

'What's that?' I ask.

'Toilet.'

The phone rings and I nearly crack a plate as it shatters my fantasy.

'Can you get that, Gem?' Mum calls from the living room.

'Yeah!' I wipe my hands on my jeans and answer it. 'Hello?'

'Gemma!' It's Treacle. She sounds worried.

'What's the matter?'

'Facebook!' she squeaks. 'Why haven't you changed your status?'

'My *status*!' A blush washes over me like a tidal wave. After all the excitement and worry of landing an actual assignment, I'd completely forgotten I hadn't changed my status from 'Marcus Bainbridge'! 'I'll ring you back in ten!' I hang up and race for the living room.

Ben's snuggled on the sofa beside Mum, pyjama-ed and physio-ed, puffing on his nebulizer. Dad's snoring in an armchair, head lolling, mouth open. He worked an extra shift today.

I whisk past them, haring for the desk in the corner and turn on the computer.

'Is everything OK?' Mum looks up, alarmed.

'Gotta change my Facebook status!' I slither the mouse back and forth on the desk, hoping to make the computer hurry up. It's taking longer than it does to wake up than Dad on a Sunday morning. 'Why do we have such an old PC!' The desktop icons slowly flash as the processor drags itself out of sleep mode and tries to get with the program.

'Sorry, love.' Mum shakes her head sympathetically. 'It's next on the list after Ben's new nebulizer.

I instantly feel bad for moaning. The compressor on his current one is on its last legs. I can hear the poor old pump

now, whining now as it struggles to push air into the nebulizer chamber – air that will turn Ben's medication into
a mist he can breathe. If it breaks altogether we'll have to
get the foot pump out and take it in turns till Dad's
worked enough shifts to buy a new one, so it's way more
important that we get a new nebulizer than a flashy PC.

I slide into the desk chair and navigate to Facebook in
two clicks and login.

There it is: my status.

Marcus Bainbridge.

I feel sick.

There are fourteen new comments underneath it.

I hope he gets the message xxx Lauren Allerton.

Look out, Marcus, you're a marked man ;) Josh Carter.

*Hey, Gem. Have you been leaving me out of the gossip
loop??!!* Sally Moore.

<3 <3 <3 <3 Ryan Edwards.

I slowly lower my head and quietly bang my forehead
on the desk.

'What's up, love?' Mum's looking round.

'Facebook disaster,' I sigh.

'Can I help?' she asks.

I shake my head without even lifting it off the smooth
pine. 'I'll sort it.' I take a deep breath and sit up. Clicking
in a fresh, uncontaminated status box, I start to type. I
decide to act causal. *Oops. Silly mistake ☺. Was searching
for Marcus and accidentally made him my status. LOL.*

I hit return and my new status slides into place at the top of my profile.

I read it. *Was searching for Marcus and accidentally made him my status.*

What am I thinking? That sounds even *worse*! Now everyone will know I was searching for his profile.

Including Marcus.

Stiff with panic, I stare at the screen, my hands hovering over the keyboard as I try to think of the perfect phrase to snatch me from the jaws of humiliation.

The desk phone rings. I pick it up before it wakes Dad. 'Yes?'

'It's me!' Savannah sounds delighted. 'This is soooo romantic! Why didn't you tell me? I had no idea. Sal's in an absolute fit. She's likes to be the first to spot a budding romance.'

'No, it's not—'

But Savannah's too busy gushing to let me get a word in. 'You'll make such a cute couple. Marcus is such a sweetie. Have you spoken to him this evening? He hasn't changed his relationships status yet. Nor have you. Are you going to do it at the same time? That'd be so romantic . . .'

I stop listening. My heart is sliding into my boots. So much for trying to get Savannah and Marcus together. My brilliant plan has gone horribly wrong. The love-missile I aimed at Marcus has turned out to be a suicide bomb.

The next morning is one of those clear, crisp March mornings that makes you think spring might happen after all.

If you hadn't just destroyed your life on Facebook.

Savannah's bouncing along beside me as we walk the bus route to school. 'So he's not asked you out, right?'

I doh-eye her. 'Why *would* he?'

'Why wouldn't he?'

'Because I'm a freaky Facebook stalker?'

Treacle's trailing behind us her giant sports bag weighing her down. 'Explain to me again why we're walking instead of bussing?'

Savannah rolls her eyes. 'We need to *talk*, of course,' she explains. 'You don't get chat-space on the number thirty-two bus.'

'Oh.' Treacle kicks a can and sends it rattling along the gutter. She spent half of last night dissecting the Marcus disaster with me on the phone after Savannah had hung up. Savannah, on the other hand, is just coming to terms with the fact that my big status announcement was a mistake – though I can't explain *why* I was searching for Marcus's profile without giving away my secret life as Jessica Jupiter and my plans for her and Marcus.

'Sorry, Treac.' I glance back

'It's OK.' Treacle looks at her watch. 'Jeff will just have to wait.'

'Bike-shed rendezvous?' Savannah spins like a terrier smelling a rabbit. 'Planned a little early-morning kissing?'

Treacle glares at her. 'Actually we're going to practise keepie-uppies.'

Savannah sighs. 'Is that all you do?'

'So, *Gem*,' Treacle says, quickly turning the spotlight back on me. 'Are you going to ask Marcus out?'

Traitor! She knows I have no interest in Marcus as boyfriend material. I zap her with my invisible death ray as Savannah turns and grabs my arm.

'Shall I soften him up for you?' she offers. 'I can give him the big sell. Tell him how nice you are. What a great girlfriend you'd make. How clever you are—'

I hold up my hands. 'Whoa! I am *not* interested in Marcus.'

'Then why the Facebook search?'

'It was for a project.' I try out the excuse I'd rehearsed with Treacle last night. 'I'm collecting birthdays. For our class. I thought it would be cool if we published a list in the webzine.'

'Oh.' Savannah looks disappointed, but not for long. 'You'd make a great couple though.' She's off again, painting dream-pictures. 'And if he hasn't asked you out yet, I can teach you a zillion ways to make sure he does.'

'Really, Savannah. No.'

'But why?' She's giving me pleading eyes. 'Marcus is a sweetie. He's so kind and thoughtful. And he's not a cabbage-brain like Ryan or Josh. When he stops being shy, he's really smart and funny. You should definitely go out with him.'

I'm surprised to hear Savannah reel off so many plus-points for Marcus. A glimmer of hope flashes through me. She knows what a nice guy Marcus is; all I have to do is convince her that he'd make a far better boyfriend than LJ.

A bunch of Year Elevens jostle past us. We're nearing the school entrance and students throng round the gates. I see Jeff watching through the fence like a chimp waiting for the banana-man. His eyes light up as he spots Treacle.

I guess it's feeding time at the zoo.

Treacle hooks her arm though mine. 'Will you be OK?' Meaning: Will you be OK if I desert you for Jeff? My heart sinks as I realize I'm going to have to face the jeering Facebook crowds de-Treacled. I bite my lip. Her eyes are glittering with hope. She's silently screaming the unspoken fear that makes ninety-nine percent of all girlfriends try too hard: girlfriends will wait, boyfriends might not.

'I'll be fine.' I give her a reassuring smile. I've got Savannah and her aura of confidence will surround us like a high-voltage force-field. Any Facebook-related comment will get fried on entry.

Treacle gives me a quick hug. 'You're a star, Gem.' She ducks into the crowds and is hanging off Jeff's arm in three seconds flat. He passes her the football he's carrying and they head away towards the playing field.

Butterflies flicker in my stomach as we head through the gates. Chelsea Leeson spots us and comes barrelling towards me. Ryan Edwards and Josh Carter are hot on her heels. I push my lips into the grin of a dead girl and fix my eyes on the school entrance.

'Marcus is over there, Gem!' Chelsea points towards the bike shed where Marcus is standing with Ryan, shifting from one foot to another, his gaze fixed on his boots.

'Thanks, Chelsea.' Savannah answers for me, her tone breezy. 'But unlike you, Gemma doesn't need to chase boys. They come to her.'

Chelsea flushes and stomps away, her mini-mob beetling after her.

'Thanks, Sav.' I squeeze her arm.

'No probs.' She flashes me a smile. 'Just keep smil—' She screeches to a halt as her gaze hits a stooping figure in the centre of the yard.

LJ.

The spring sunshine flashes off his hair gel. He's surrounded by Year Ten girls all paying court like he's
Henry VIII. As we watch, he unpeels his shirt and starts
counting his six pack. I wait for one of his audience to
swoon. But they stay standing, their eyes popping like
steamrollered bubble-wrap.

'I wonder if he's remembered my name?' Before I know
it, Savannah is trying to drag me towards the group of
girls.

I yank her back.

'What?' She stares at me.

'I've been reading an article,' I lie quickly. I've got to
do something before she makes a total idiot of herself
by throwing herself at LJ in front of an audience. 'It
says boys are more likely to fall for girls who are a chal-
lenge.'

'Are you saying I'm easy?' Savannah puts her hands on
her hips.

'No!' I backtrack. 'I'm just saying, play it cool.'

'Since when did you give relationship advice?'

'Like I said, I read it in an article.' I grab a statistic
from the air. 'Eighty-four percent of all relationships start
with an insult.'

Savannah narrows her eyes. 'Really?'

I've got her hooked. 'Yes. Just be rude, act aloof, as
though he's the last boy in the world you'd bother with.'

'And that will get him interested in me?' She sounds unconvinced.

'He'll be so hot for you, you'll have to wear oven gloves.' I smile in what I hope is a convincing way.

While Savannah digests, the first bell rings. LJ recovers his six-pack and his fan club begins to drift schoolward.

Savannah hoists her bag on to her shoulder and heads towards the front entrance, sweeping past LJ with impressive indifference.

'Hey!' he calls as her bag buffets him.

She turns, frowning. 'Are you talking to me?' I never knew Savannah could sound so cold. She's Dr Freeze.

LJ looks confused, like a dog expecting a biscuit and getting a worm pill. 'You're climate-zone girl, aren't you?'

Savannah tips her head, not missing a beat. 'As far as you're concerned, I'm the Arctic.'

Wow. I watch her walk away, glowing with pride. Then I see LJ's eyes spark into life. *No!* For the first time, those dark brown pools have snapped into focus. He looks interested. A small smile curls his lips as he watches Savannah skip up the school steps.

What have I done?

I race after Savannah, catching up at the top of the stairs. I try to block her view, but it's too late. She's staring back across the yard, her gaze locked with LJ's.

She breaks it off. 'Oh, Gem! You're a genius! Did you

see him staring at me. I've really got his attention now.' She's overjoyed.

I'm gutted. Another plan backfired. I'm the opposite of genius.

Then I spot Jeff and Treacle wandering arm in arm across the fast-emptying playground. They're gazing sappily into each other's eyes, meandering like drunks over the tarmac.

Maybe there's hope. After all, I got it right with Jeff and Treacle. Perhaps, in the end, I'll do the same for Savannah and Marcus.

☆ ☆ ☆

'Turn it down a bit!' I yell over the racket of Ben's Xbox.

Ben flashes me a death-glare but lowers the volume.

Once Sonic the Hedgehog isn't making the ornaments rattle, I try again. 'Will's going to make it as hard for me as he can, I just know it.'

'Don't let him bully you.' Treacle's slouching on the armchair opposite, pulling a post-pizza muffin apart and filling her cheeks. She's come round to help me babysit Ben while Mum and Dad are feasting at the local gastropub. Not that I need help. I'm a world-expert on Ben. I know that in exchange for forty minutes uninterrupted Xbox he'll give in gracefully to physio, meds and bedtime. Especially if I airplane him from Xbox to physio-table to bed, while he machine-guns invisible aliens.

I check my watch. Thirty minutes of Xboxing to go. 'I'm not so worried about him bossing me about,' I confess. 'I'm worried he won't let me work on the article at all. When Mr Harris told him he had to let me help, I thought he was going to strangle Cindy, then beat me to death with her cold, dead body.'

Treacle laughs, spraying a mouthful of muffin crumbs. 'I can see why you want to be a journalist,' she says, dabbing up the mess. 'You do have tendency to thrive on drama.'

I ignore the slur. 'But he looked really angry.'

Treacle sits up. 'Let's not brand him a psycho-killer yet,' she says sensibly.

'OK.' I sweep reality under the carpet. 'Let's pretend he's a sweet, helpful, generous guy who *wants* me to help.' I chew at my thumbnail. 'But what if I mess it up? This is my big chance to prove I can do some real journalism. What if I can't? What if I just follow him around saying stuff so dumb I prove him right?'

Treacle gulps down the last of her muffin. 'But, Gemma, you rock as a writer! Cindy gave you the horoscopes and you've made them the talk of the school. You're going to do the same with this article.'

I'm grateful, but unconvinced. 'But I'm such a klutz around Will. He turns me into a quivering wreck. I'll never be able to think straight with him snapping at me and pointing out every tiny mistake.'

'Fair enough.' Treacle brushes the crumbs from her jersey into the palm of her hand and drops them into the bin beside her chair. 'Let's practise.'

I frown. 'Practise what?'

'You made me role-play meeting Jeff's parents.' She stands up. 'Let's role-play you working with Will Bold.'

'The Jeff role-play didn't turn out too well,' I remind her.

'Yes, but once you'd demonstrated just how horrible it could be, I felt ready for anything. I still do. You've totally prepared me for Friday night.' She straightens up. 'There's no way Jeff's mother will be as awful as you.'

'Hey!' I object.

She grins and hauls me to my feet. 'Come on. I'll be Will.' She rolls her shoulders forward and drops her chin. 'Right, Gemma,' she growls, 'I suppose I'm stuck with you. We'd better start work.'

'What do you want me to do, Will?' I ask eagerly.

Treacle breaks character, 'No! no! You have to play it cool. You're not a puppy trying to please. You're a reporter looking for a story.'

I nod, shaking out my arms in an attempt to loosen up. I remind myself of the advice I gave Savannah. *Act aloof, as though he's the last boy in the world you'd bother with.*

'Let's try it again.' Treacle jerks me from my thoughts.

I nod. 'Ready.'

'Have your brought your notebook?'

I sniff carelessly. 'Yeah.'

'Pen?'

'Will this do?' I slide out a pencil I'd lodged in my curls when I was doing some homework earlier.

'Neat trick.' Treacle rubs her nose. 'OK, start taking notes.'

I hold out my pretend pad and real pencil and wait for dictation.

Treacle starts. 'So Slider's holding three corners, selling one hundred, two hundred caps a day, slicing a piece off the top of every sale, and Juicy finds out, takes offence and decides to make a hit . . .' Treacle's obviously been watching US cop shows again.

I scratch my ear with my pencil. 'So we're tailing Juicy?'

She looks at me, managing to pull off a perfect Will Bold sneer. 'Juicy? Why would we tail Juicy? It's Slider who's got the brains.'

'So we tail Slider?' I ask, trying to keep up.

'Why would we tail Slider? He's just taken a hit. Are you listening to a word I'm saying?'

I start to fluster. Her Will impersonation is too good. I feel like an idiot.

'So who *are* we tailing?'

'Who said anything about tailing?'

The Xbox goes quiet. Ben's hanging over the back of

the sofa, watching. 'Are you playing cops and robbers? Can I play?'

Treacle slides him a look. 'Sure, Shorty. But we're reporters, not cops, and we're about to bust a case wide open.' Her gaze flicks back to me. 'If my idiot assistant can keep up.'

Ben clambers over the sofa, lining up beside Treacle. 'Yeah, Gem. Keep up.'

My heartrate's climbing. 'I'm trying.'

'Then read it back,' Treacle orders.

'Read *what* back?'

'You were taking notes,' Treacle reminds me with a Will-style snort.

'Oh, yeah.' I remember the imaginary notepad. 'Slidey was making caps and the juice was taking hits . . .'

'Hey, Shorty.' Treacle nods at Ben. '*You* make the notes. Girl Friday's pencil seems to be running on unleaded.'

'Yes, sir!' Ben snatches my pencil and starts making pretend notes.

'Hey! That's my job!' I snatch it back.

'Treacle wants *me* to do it!' Ben makes a grab for the pencil. I hang on to it and we tussle to the ground, squawking. As I finally pin Ben down and uncurl his fingers from the precious pencil, I notice Treacle's foot tapping beside us.

'Quite finished, Stone?' She's peering down her nose at me.

I scramble to my feet. 'Sorry about that. I was just getting my pencil.' I hold up my imaginary notebook again. 'Ready.'

Treacle rolls her eyes. 'Note-taking's over, Stone, we've got real work to do now.'

'What?'

'Do I have to think of everything?' Will-Treacle snaps.

Ben's on his feet. 'I know. Let's find some evidence.'

Will-Treacle pats him on the head. 'Good thinking, little guy.'

My blood boils with frustration. 'That's not fair. This is my role-play!'

Treacle pushes up her sleeves. 'No time for playing, Stone. There's work to be done.'

I begin to object. 'But you said—'

'If I said "jump off a bridge" would you do it?'

'I wouldn't!' Ben shouts.

'Nor me!' I chime in.

Treacle tips her head. 'But what if we're undercover and we just got busted and it's the only way out?'

'Oh! I don't know, I . . .' My head is spinning. Too much, too fast. 'I don't know!' I slam down on to the sofa, arms crossed tight.

Treacle drops the act and slumps to the floor. Sitting at my feet, she looks up at me earnestly. 'I think we should drop the role-play,' she suggests. 'Improv's clearly not our thing.'

Ben looks crestfallen. 'Awww. It was fun!'

I reach out and ruffle his hair. 'Go play Xbox,' I tell him. 'I'm starting your physio in twenty minutes.'

'OK.' Ben clambers back over the sofa and drops down in front of the TV.

Defeated, I grab a cushion and hug it. 'He's going to kill me.'

'Who? Ben?' Treacle blinks.

'No, Will.' I sigh. 'Why on earth did I ask if I could work with him?' A cloud of despair floats across the room and settles above my head. 'He's going to totally annihilate me and use my blood as printer ink.'

My despair cloud's not exactly lifted by the morning, but I've wrestled it down to a mini-cloud I can fit in my pocket and take to school with me.

It's Wednesday: publication day. The webzine will be hitting everyone's school email around lunchtime.

The morning drags and, by the time lunchtime actually arrives, I'm starving. I'm the only person I know who gets hungry from worrying. I'm also the only person I know who carries despair-clouds in her pockets.

I sit down at the lunch table with Treacle, Savannah and Sally Moore, happy to be lost in the lunch room hubbub.

'Have you checked out your stars yet?' Savannah's got a new smartphone and she's scrolling through her email while the rest of us munch our sandwiches.

Sally leans over and peeks at the screen. 'What does Jessica say today?'

I chew my tuna sub and watch Savannah's face as she scans her horoscope. Will she get the anti-LJ message?

She starts reading out loud: '*You may think you've found*

your heart's desire but, my dear Fin-derella, your Prince Charming may turn out to be all charm and no prince.'

Savannah sniffs. 'Wow, Jessica's a bit out of date this week,' she scoffs. 'She's still talking about Josh.'

No, she's not!

'Yeah well, she was right about him and she still is.' Sally stares hard across the lunch room to where Chelsea and Josh are cosied up at a table, sharing crisps.

'I know, but you'd think she'd have realized I've moved on since then,' Savannah replies. 'Maybe she's ill or something.' She looks at me. 'Is she ill?'

'How should I know?' I say a little too defensively. Under the table, Treacle gives my foot a kick.

"Ummm . . . I mean, she never actually *comes in* to the school. She's a friend of Cindy's dad . . . She used to do the horoscopes on the paper he edited. She emails her column over to us every week. I have no idea where she is. Or who she is,' I splutter, my heart pounding.

Treacle kicks me again. Harder. I cling on to my tuna sub like it's a life raft.

'All right, all right, calm down,' Savannah says. 'I'm sure she'll catch up with the new man in my life eventually.' Her gaze flashes to the doorway, where LJ appears like a summoned genie.

Treacle slides down behind her sandwich. 'Saved by Prince Charming,' she mutters.

My heart rate slows back to normal, even if I do think LJ is a total loser at least his arrival seems to have distracted Savannah from questioning me any further about Jessica Jupiter. 'How does she *not* get that *he's* Prince Charm*less*?' I whisper to Treacle.

'She doesn't want to get it,' Treacle murmurs back.

'Oh. My. God!' Sally's gabbling. 'He's coming over.'

Savannah instantly slips into cool mode, fixing her gaze and pretending she's not aware that a god is descending from the heavens. Crowds part to let LJ pass as he heads for our table. A small entourage of angelic Year Tens flutter after him.

I quickly wrap my foot around the empty chair at the end, but LJ tugs it free and sits down. 'Hi.' His ultra-white, super-toothed smile is aimed directly at Savannah.

Bethany Richards – the only Year Ten to rival Cindy in plastic good looks – grabs the empty seat beside LJ and sits down.

The rest of the entourage settle around us too, perching on the edge of the table and backs of chairs like Trafalgar Square pigeons.

Savannah slides LJ a look but doesn't speak.

Sally does. 'Hi, LJ.' She sounds so grateful for his presence I want to wretch.

Instead, I snatch a bite of my sandwich. Treacle's watching through slitted eyes as LJ unclicks the lid of his

67

sushi box. He takes out a pair of chopsticks and taps them on the table before picking out a piece of fish. 'Is that a chicken sandwich?' he asks Savannah, before popping the raw sea-flesh into his mouth.

'Uh-huh.' Savannah takes a bite.

'Back home, no one mixes protein and carbs any more.' He swallows. 'It's the fastest way to put on weight and destroy your dermalayer.'

Treacle looks at me. 'He means *skin*, right?'

I shrug. We need Cindy to translate. She'd love this conversation. I wonder suddenly if LJ inspired her eat-yourself-pretty article.

Bethany leans across the table and pats Treacle's arm. 'Sporty types like you don't need to worry,' she says reassuringly.

Treacle nearly coughs up her dinner. 'What's that supposed to mean?'

Bethany smiles sweetly. 'You're more about muscle tone than good looks, so you can eat anything you like.'

Treacle growls in my ear. 'I'll show her some muscle tone in a minute.'

I'm less worried about Treacle folding Bethany into an origami napkin than I am about Savannah's reaction to LJ's comment. She's put down her sandwich and started eating an apple instead.

I watch her nibble and take a defiant bite of my tuna sub. No vain boy is going to put me off my food.

LJ's comfortable now, foot up on Bethany's chair, chatting and laughing with his entourage.

Savannah is staring at the tabletop, sucking on her apple like a Hollywood princess with an eating disorder.

'Are you coming?' I pack up my lunch box. 'Treacle? Sav?'

Savannah shakes her head.

'We're not finished,' Sal rattles a packet of chilli rice crackers at me.

Treacle shoves her sandwich box in her backpack. 'I am.'

As we head for the door, the entourage ruffle feathers, fighting over our empty chairs. I glance back at them in dismay. 'I can't believe Sav dumped her sandwich just because LJ—' *Slam!* I walk straight into someone.

'Look out!' Marcus brushes me away, looking flustered.

'S-sorry!' This is all I need. I managed to get through the whole of yesterday and this morning without looking at Marcus; even though we share every lesson except Geography, our gaze managed to avoid crashing across a crowded classroom. I don't know what he thinks about my Facebook blunder and I don't *want* to know. But as I stare at him, blushing, I realize I'm about to find out.

He's blinking at me, a frozen look on his face like he's just stepped into traffic. 'Oh, hi,' he says awkwardly.

Swallow me, Earth. Just open up and swallow me whole.

The Earth ignores me.

'Gemma . . .' he begins.

'It's OK. I know.' It's *not* OK and I *don't* know; I just want to stop him. There's nothing he can say that I want to hear.

'It's just,' Marcus presses on, 'it's not that I don't like you, or there's any reason not to like you, except that . . .' his blush intensifies.

I kind of feel sorry for him. 'The whole status thing was an accident!' I blurt out.

'Good!' he blurts back. 'I mean not "good", just I'm glad, because I sort of like someone else.'

'Of course you do.' Did that sound bitter? 'I mean it's OK because I just put you in my status by mistake. I was actually doing a search. For birthdays. Because I'm – er – I'm – er . . .' I try out the same lie I tried on Savannah. But this time I stall. I sound so lame. He's going to know I'm lying. 'There really was a good reason for searching for you. Honest.' I'm babbling, 'I don't just randomly search for boys. Not that I searched for you on purpose. I mean—'

Treacle grabs my elbow. 'Come on, Gem. Or we'll be late for the thing.'

'Yeah.' Relief floods me as she drags me past Marcus. Then, for some reason only a really stupid person would understand, I glance back at him. 'Bye, Marcus.'

'*Shut up!*' Treacle grabs my hand as I perform a lame wave.

As we reach the safety of the corridor, my shoulders droop. 'He's going to think I like him, isn't he?'

Treacle sucks air through her teeth. 'You didn't exactly play it cool,' she admits. 'It was like your Jessica Jupiter jabbering in the canteen all over again!'

'Shoot me,' I beg. 'Put me out of my misery.'

'Later,' she promises. She looks at her watch. 'I'm meeting Jeff on the pitch. Come with me?'

I shake my head. 'I'll go and do some work on the webzine.' Hiding in the storeroom sounds like a better idea than being anywhere in public right now.

Treacle looks worried. 'Are you sure? Jeff won't mind.'

I'm not up to making small talk with Jeff. 'Thanks, but I want to see if Jessica's got any fan mail.' I force a smile.

Treacle shrugs. 'OK.' She gives me a sudden hug. 'Don't worry about Marcus. I bet he's flattered really. It's just that he's still hooked on Sav.'

'I wish she was hooked on him and not LJ.'

'Go and start work on her horoscope for next week,' Treacle encourages. 'And this time, don't be so subtle.'

'I'll type with a sledgehammer,' I promise, heading for the stairs.

As I near Webzine HQ I hear Sam's guitar. It sounds really good. I can tell he's been practising. 'Nice riff,' I tell him as I enter and park my bag.

He looks up, his pensive frown smoothing. 'Thanks.'

Behind me, a keyboard is rattling beneath thundering fingers. Only one person types that intensely. 'Hi, Will.' I turn round. He's got his head down, hammering out words at a hundred miles an hour. He doesn't answer. *Great*. I can see we're going to work really well together.

'He's been like that for fifteen minutes,' Sam tells me.

'Doesn't he need to eat?' I wonder.

'I guess not.' He leans his guitar against the wall behind him. 'Are you busy Friday night?'

I'm never busy Friday night. 'Not really.'

He slides something from his back pocket. 'I've got a spare ticket,' he says, turning over a thin blue strip in his fingers 'For our Sounds gig.'

'I thought it was sold out.' Savannah's been trying to get hold of tickets since Monday but it seems like the school's already bought out the gig.

'I get a few extra.' He stares at the ticket thoughtfully and I wonder if he really wants to give it to me.

'If you'd rather give it to someone else—' I begin.

'No.' He thrusts it at me. 'I figure you've heard me talking about the new set for so long, you deserve to hear it.' He half looks at me then sits down and grabs his guitar.

'Thanks, Sam.' I'm flattered. I thought he'd save his tickets for his Year Ten friends. They must have tickets already. 'I'm really looking forward to hear—'

'Gemma,' Will interrupts.

I spin, surprised. 'What?'

'Do you want to start helping me on this article?' he asks.

I wonder if there's a hidden camera in the room. Why does he suddenly seem fine with me helping him? It must be a set up. Some kind of experiment to see what happens if you snatch the Invisibility Cloak off a Year Nine without warning.

'Well?' he growls. His dark gaze turns all Voldemort.

My brain shuts down. Except for the huge, dumb bit that controls my mouth. 'I'm really looking forward to working with you. I'm just so happy you agreed to let me help. I promise I'll do my best. I really want to –'

'Yeah, whatever.' He shuts me up. 'Do you want to know what the story's about?'

'The story?' I've turned into a parrot.

'You ... know ...' Will slows his speech like I'm French. 'The ... story ... you're ... going ... to ... help ... me ... with.'

Sam's chair scrapes behind me. The sudden noise jumpstarts my brain. 'Yes!' I say. 'The story. Yes!'

Will stares past me at Sam. 'We need privacy though.'

Sam sniffs. 'I get the message.' Swinging his guitar, he lopes out of the room.

Will closes the door after him.

'I'm really happy you've agreed to let me help.' I'm gabbling again.

'So you said already.' Will starts pacing. 'Let's agree you're pleased and get on with it.'

He's breezing back and forth past me. I feel like I'm watching tennis.

'First—' He stops suddenly. 'You have to swear to keep this secret.'

'Secret?' I think back to my dishes daydream about the warehouse and human trafficking. 'Is it dangerous?' Excitement prickles my skin.

'Could be.' Will starts pacing again. 'You're going to need to keep your cool.' He puts the brakes on and leans toward me. 'You can do that, right?' He frowns. 'If you have to?'

'Yes,' I promise, hoping it's true. I've never faced a really dangerous situation before. What if I lose my cool? What if I end up a quivering wreck who can't even hold a torch straight?

'OK then.' He sits back on a desk and stretches out his legs. 'You swear?'

'Sometimes,' I confess, 'but not really bad words.'

He gives me a wake-up-you-idiot look. 'Not that kind of swear,' he snaps. 'Do you swear to keep what I'm about to tell you secret?'

I catch up, blushing. 'Yes,' I say hurriedly. 'Absolutely. Scout's honour.'

'Great.' Will starts tapping his foot. 'I have a girl scout for a partner. This is what Watergate must have been like.'

'What?'

'Watergate,' he repeats. 'Woodward and Bernstein? President Nixon? Secret tapes?'

It rings a bell but I can't place it. 'Like the X-Files?'

'Look,' he sighs. 'Just Google it when you get home. Right now I need you to listen. We're going to be working on a story about Sounds.'

I stare at him.

'The nightclub?' Will reaches forward and raps his knuckles lightly on my head. 'Where lover-boy's gigging on Friday night?'

'Oh yeah.' I try and focus. Why am I acting so dumb? I need to speed up or I'm always going to be three strokes behind his thought-wave.

Will glances at the door and lowers his voice to a conspiratorial whisper. 'There's a rumour that the owner, Dave Wiggins, is using it as a front for some seriously dodgy dealing. And we're going to find out what's really going on.'

'*Dodgy?*' I twitch like a corpse taking a zillion volts. 'How do you know?' This could be a *real* story, not just some pull-out section on homework techniques or lunch-room etiquette.

Will scratches his nose. 'I've got a source,' he says meaningfully. 'He used to work at Sounds.'

'But he doesn't he work there any more?' My brain's fully engaged now.

'He got fired.'

'Can you trust him?' I ask. 'He might have a grudge against the person who fired him.'

'That's possible,' Will concedes. 'That's why we need to get in there and find evidence.'

He said *we*! 'Evidence of what?'

'My source claims he's heard Wiggins making phone calls to some pretty crooked business associates. Guys who've done time.'

'In prison?'

'No.' Will snorts. 'Disney World.'

His snarky comment bounces off me. I'm too busy

thinking. 'Is that all we have? A disgruntled employee who claims he heard Wiggins phone an ex-con.' I sit on the desk opposite Will's. 'Is that enough?'

'There've been weird deliveries,' Will goes on. 'After hours. It's enough to get my nose twitching. Sounds is launching these underage nights, which every teenager in town wants to go to. If there's something criminal going on there, the public should know.'

'So what do you want me to do?' I reach for my bag and slide out a jotter, ready to take notes.

'You'll be at Sounds this Friday,' Will tells me. 'I want you to get Sam to take you backstage.'

'Why don't *you* get Sam to take you backstage?'

'I couldn't get tickets,' Will says bluntly. 'I've been looking for a way in.'

'And I'm it.'

'You're it.' Will's the parrot now.

Disappointment drops like a stone into my stomach. That's why he suddenly wants me on the story. Because Sam gave me a ticket. I resist the urge to tell him to do his own dirty work. This is my chance. So what if Will is just using me as a spy because he's got no other option? If I can uncover something at the gig, he'll *have* to start taking me seriously.

Will goes on. 'Just get Sam to take you backstage and have a look around. Make a note of anything suspicious.'

'Why would Sam take me backstage?'

'He gave you the ticket, didn't he?'

'Only because it was spare,' I argue. 'I'm not his special guest or anything.'

Will stands up. 'Then give it to me and I'll ask Sam to show me backstage.'

I narrow my eyes. There's no way I'm letting Will snatch this chance. 'No, I'll do it.'

'Good.' Will reaches for his backpack and pulls out a scrap of paper. 'I want you to see if you can find Wiggins' office. Keep your ears open. If you see him, watch him. And if anything seems out of place, make a note.'

I wonder how I'm meant to know what's in place or out of place. The only backstage I've ever seen was a church hall when I was eight and starring as Fairy Number Three in Miss Duvall's ballet troupe.

I'm going to have to trust my instinct and hope Sam doesn't mind a nosey Year Nine trailing after him. He'll understand when the story comes out. *If* it comes out. Right now it's just gossip.

Will's scribbling on his scrap of paper. He hands it to me. 'Here's my number. Text me yours and phone me if you need to.'

There's a loud cough from the doorway. We both turn and see Sam standing there. 'I forgot my plectrum,' he mutters, going over to the desk.

I stare down at the phone number, fingers trembling.

Behind me, the door slams shut. Sam's left and Will ducks out behind him. I'm buzzing with excitement. I'm going to turn gossip into a real news story. If there's evidence that Sounds is a cover for criminal activity, I'll find it.

I slide behind a desk and switch on the PC. I'm picturing my byline next to Will's: *Exclusive by Will Bold and Gemma Stone*. This could be the break that launches my career; the first step to winning a global award and international acclaim. The crowds are cheering in my head as I hold up the trophy. 'Thank you! Thank you!' A small huddle of women and children are sobbing in the front row. My exposé has freed them from a life of slavery and exploitation. I'm just grateful for the chance to have changed their lives.

'Gemma?'

I nearly fall off my chair as Cindy skids into the room.

Her blonde bob's flapping and there's an excited flush in her cheeks. 'Was that Will leaving? Has he briefed you yet?'

I nod dumbly.

'So you know about the story?'

I nod again.

'Well?' She's leaning in, eyes bright. 'What is it?'

I shift in my chair. 'It's secret.'

'Oh per-*leazzze*!' She frowns like I've thwarted her evil scheme to take over the world. I half expect her to rush to the window and summon her army of winged mon-keys.

First I'm eye-speared by Voldemort, now the Wicked Witch of the West is grilling me. I think I preferred it when Will and Cindy just ignored me.

She flings her bag down. 'What was the point of put-ting you on the story if you don't dish the dirt?'

'I thought you were trying to annoy Will,' I mutter, 'not spy on him.'

'Annoying him was just a bonus.' Cindy starts rooting in her bag, her smooth-as-silk forehead crumpling. I rec-ognize the look; she's concentrating. I guess that she's fumbling for samples for her beauty column. I say a silent prayer: *Don't dump them on me.* With horoscopes to write *and* Will's story to work on, there's no way I'll have time to give her feedback on this week's war-paint.

I hit shutdown and grab my bag. 'Got to go,' I say quickly. 'Treacle's waiting.'

'But—'

I don't hear the rest. I'm out the door and haring down the hallway.

'You'll never guess!' Savannah ambushes me outside our form room.

'You're right. I won't.' I don't have time for guessing games. My mind's whirling with plans for my Friday-night undercover assignment at Sounds.

Savannah's hanging off my arm, her green eyes bright. 'Pleeeeeaaase guess.'

'LJ?'

'Yes, yes, yes!'

'He asked you out.' I say the most ludicrous thing I can think of.

'Yes!' Savannah is jubilant.

No!

My disappointment doesn't register on Savannah's mood scale; she's too close to ecstasy to notice. 'He's asked me to the gig at Sounds on Friday night!' She bounces round like Tigger on a sugar rush.

What about Marcus? I think, she'll never notice him now. Not even if Jessica Jupiter spells his name out in flashing stars.

Savannah waves a familiar blue strip of paper in my face. 'You should have seen the look on Bethany's face when LJ gave me this ticket and told me he'd see me at Sounds on Friday.'

Hope glints like a diamond in my pit of despair. 'So he didn't actually ask you out on a date?'

Savannah blinks at me. 'It's as good as a date.' She waves the ticket again. 'He didn't give a ticket to Bethany, did he?'

'She might already have one,' I point out.

'Why are you being such a doom-merchant?' Savannah loses her bounce and stares at me.

'Sorry.' Upsetting Savannah isn't my plan. I slide the ticket Sam gave me out of my pocket and show her. 'I'm going too!' I flash her a smile.

She grasps my hand. 'Where on earth did you get it! These are like gold dust!'

'Sam,' I tell her.

She looks at me from beneath her lashes like I've just admitted I'm Batman. '*Really?*' She says, using her meaningful voice.

'It's his gig,' I point out. 'He's probably got too many tickets and needs to unload some.'

Savannah raises an eyebrow. 'Whatever you say, Gem.' She flicks her hair over her shoulder. 'You know what this means though?'

'What?' I try and guess where Savannah's butterfly mind is fluttering to now.

'We can *get ready together!*' she squeals.

Treacle bobs round the corner, glossy black hair wind-blown, cheeks rosy from the chilly football field. 'Get ready for what?'

Savannah shows Treacle our tickets. 'We're both going on Friday night!'

Treacle slumps against the form-room door. 'I wish I was going to the gig instead of meeting Jeff's parents.'

Savannah starts bouncing again. 'You could *get ready with us!*' she gasps. 'Then we can give you moral support, and you can help Gemma with her hair.' She glances at my curls, wild now the morning straightening has worn off. 'I don't think I can manage it alone.' She gives me a wicked grin.

Treacle hugs me protectively. 'Gem's hair is gorgeous,' she protests. 'Her wild, windswept look is cool.'

Savannah tips her head. 'Less windswept, more hurricane survivor!'

'Hey!' I belt her with my bag and she escapes squealing into the classroom.

'Help me!'

I chase her in, ignoring her pleas for mercy until she cowers behind a desk. Marcus, feet up on a chair, is leafing through a comic at the back of the classroom. 'Do you need assistance?'

Savannah looks up eagerly. 'Yes!'

Marcus winks. 'I was talking to Gemma, not you.' He sounds relaxed. Like he's deleted our lunchtime soap-opera moment. Savannah gawps at him while I collapse into relieved giggles and spare her life.

We calm down and settle in our usual spot beside the radiator. Treacle clings on to it, breathing in the rising heat.

Savannah stretches out her long legs. 'Friday is going to be so great.'

Treacle looks at her doubtfully. 'For you, maybe.'

I bite my lip. Doubt creeps into my mind. What if LJ ignores Sav completely and she's devastated? Or, even worse, makes a move on her? What if I fail to find anything to report back to Will? He'll never take me seriously and I'll be stuck on the horoscopes for life. I start chewing my thumbnail, suddenly worried. Friday night might turn out to be anything but great.

'How are we going to make Sav look terrible?' Treacle is sitting on my bed, reviewing my brilliant plan to bomb Savannah's chances with LJ.

It's Friday night and the bus leaves in an hour. I look at my watch. Savannah's fifteen minutes late. If she doesn't arrive soon, there won't be time to turn her from beauty to beast.

'Savannah's way too pretty,' Treacle points out. 'She'd even look great in *this*!' She looks down at the caramel cardigan and neat turquoise dogtooth checked skirt she's borrowed from her mother.

Jeff's parents will think he's dating a librarian.

I peer out the window at the empty street. 'We've made you look like Ugly Betty,' I argue. 'We can do it with Sav too.'

My bedroom is awash with discarded clothes. Treacle's tried on everything I own, but decided in the end caramel and turquoise is the only way to go.

My outfit was easy to choose. I'm not trying to impress anyone. I'm just after a good story so all I need are trainers for creeping around backstage, a pocket for my phone, and jeans so I can climb out a window in an emergency.

I check my watch again. She's sixteen minutes late now. 'Hurry up, Sav!'

'Are you sure this is fair?' Treacle asks me, a worried look on her face.

'It's the only way I can think of to save her from LJ.'

'Does she need saving?' Treacle suddenly seems doubtful. 'She really likes LJ.'

'I know,' I concede. 'But the only person LJ really likes is himself. We're just trying to protect her.'

'Perhaps he'll be different with Savannah,' Treacle says. 'He did give her a ticket.'

'I bet he gave tickets to his whole fan club.'

The doorbell goes and I shoot out on to the landing. 'Savannah!'

She's hammering upstairs. 'Sorry I'm late,' she puffs. 'Forgot to switch on the hair straightners. I spent ten minutes trying to flatten my hair with sub-zero GHDs!' She races past me, a designer carrier bag trailing, and disappears into my room.

Poor Sav. She must be in a state to make such a basic fashion error. I follow her into my room. The carrier bag's on the floor and she's already holding up two stunning outfits.

'Which one?' She wafts an electric blue tulip dress in

front of her. It's fabulous. Then she does a quick switch and dangles a sequined sheath dress under her chin. The spangles light her up like a goddess.

'Neither.' I snatch them from her quickly. 'You'll look the same as the rest of his groupies.'

She gapes at me. 'But they're my best outfits.'

'And they're beautiful.' I lay them carefully on the bed. 'But what if Bethany's there. You know she's going to go for the same leggy, knock-out look. You need to stand out.'

Savannah's face crumples with doubt. 'Do you think so?' She looks at Treacle.

Treacle nods. 'Gemma's right.' She picks up a long beige dress from the floor. 'Try this. It's slinky.'

It *is* figure-hugging but we're hoping the mushroom sheen will make Savannah invisible.

She slides it on and turns round to check the mirror. 'Not bad . . .'

Not *bad*? It clings to her from neck to ankle. She looks *fabulous*, like a lotus flower about to blossom. 'No good.' I grab a grey, boxy, knee-length dress that should turn her into a dowdy secretary.

'Really?' Savannah's still admiring the lotus dress. 'I quite like this one.'

'You'll love this one more,' I promise, holding out the grey dress.

She takes it uncertainly. 'Won't I look like a frump?'

Treacle raises her eyebrows at me. I know what's she's thinking. Savannah's un-frumpable.

She tries on the grey dress. I'm right; she looks like a secretary, but a secretary who's just whipped off her specs and let down her hair to reveal her inner beauty queen. If anything, the dullness of the dress highlights her gorgeousness.

Treacle stares in dismay. 'It's not fair.' She stands next to Savannah in her librarian outfit. 'We're like Before and After photos.'

I herd Treacle away. 'This is not a good time for comparisons. You're visiting Aged Relatives. Savannah's spending the evening with the King of Cool.' Then an idea flashes in my brain.

Emo!

LJ – an all-American, catwalk-worshipping, hair-gel-based life-form – is bound to think that the dark, troubled world of a classic emo is totally without Cool. But how can I sell it to Savannah?

'I know!' I cry.

'What?' Treacle and Savannah goggle at me.

'Cindy's been doing a survey on what boys think are the hottest looks.' OK, it's a complete lie, but Savannah's leaning closer, eyes wide, so I keep going. 'As beauty editor on the webzine, Cindy is trying to discover what fashion-look gets the most attention from boys aged fourteen to sixteen.'

Savannah claps her hands excitedly. 'That's LJ's age-group.'

'Precisely.'

Treacle tips her head. 'Well?'

I press on. 'Out of all the boys she surveyed . . .' I wait for an imaginary drum-roll '. . . the most popular look is . . .'

Savannah's practically panting.

'. . . *emo*.'

'Emo?' Savannah echoes the word like she's mis-heard.

I cross my fingers behind my back and pray she takes the bait.

'Emo,' she says again. She starts nodding. '*Emo*.' It's sinking in. 'OK. I'll give it a try.'

I give Treacle a massive thumbs up behind Savannah's back. We're going to make her look grunge-tastic.

Treacle starts working on her make-up while I find every piece of black clothing I own. When I turn round, arms loaded, Treacle's already rimmed Savannah's eyes with red eyeshadow and is working on a thick lining of black.

I wait while she adds the finishing touches: whitening Savannah's complexion till it's vampire-pale and then mixing Savannah's crimson lipstick with a drop of eye-liner to make a lip-stain so dark it's scary.

'Now for the clothes,' I smile.

Between us, we manage to cover most of Savannah. We swathe her, head to foot in black. Ripped tights, tight dress, all swamped by a flowing coat I borrowed from Mum three years ago when it was already fit for the recycling bin. I've got some purple hairspray left over from Halloween to tint a few strands around Savannah's face.

I look at my watch. Finished with five minutes to spare.

'What do you think?' Treacle asks as Savannah looks in the mirror.

Personally, I love it. She's a gothic nightmare. Dracula would eat her up. But clean-cut, carb-cutting LJ will recoil in horror.

'I look a bit pale.' Savannah pinches her cheeks. She doesn't look entirely in love with the style-change.

'Come on.' I start hustling her toward the door before she bails. 'We don't want to miss the bus.'

Treacle gasps. 'I've got to be at Jeff's in fifteen minutes.' She's first downstairs and out the front door.

I follow with Savannah, ushering her after Treacle before I poke my head round the kitchen door.

Mum looks up from the stove where she's stirring risotto. 'Are you off?'

'Got to catch the bus.'

'What about dinner?'

'Save me some,' I tell her. 'I won't be late.'

'Half past ten,' she calls as I head for the front door.

'OK,' I yell back.

Ben is standing in the living-room doorway, staring after Savannah as she flutters out of the house like a bat. 'Is it a fancy dress party?' he asks.

'Shh!' I'm terrified Savannah will hear. 'It's just a look she's trying out.'

Ben looks thoughtful. 'She doesn't look pretty any more.'

I wave him away, secretly pleased. 'I'll see you in the morning, Ben.' Before he can say anything else I follow Treacle and Savannah on to the driveway.

'Bye, Treac!' I say as we part at the corner. 'Good luck.'

Treacle wanders away, shoulders drooping as she heads for Jeff's.

'You'll be fine!' I shout after her.

'Don't forget to smile!' Savannah calls.

Savannah and I head for the bus stop, arriving just as the bus does. '*You* mustn't smile,' I tell her as we get onboard. 'Smiling isn't part of the look.'

Swaying as we head upstairs to find seats, I start to feel like a freak next to Sav. I look stupidly normal by comparison and I'm kind of embarrassed to be seen with her. Guilt pricks me and, when I spot Marcus with Ryan, Bilal, Sal and Chris McClaren at the back of the top deck, I feel even worse.

'Oh my God!' Sal comes racing down the aisle. 'What have you done to yourself, Sav?'

I cringe. *Shut up, Sal. It's for her own good!*

'What?' Savannah's blinking at her.

'You *do* know LJ will be there, don't you?'

Savannah flicks a purple strand of hair over her shoulder. 'Well, duh!'

'So why are you dressed like Kurt Cobain just died again?' Sal is clearly in shock.

'I'm trying out a new look.' She gazes at me fondly. 'Gemma told me boys think it's hot.'

Sally looks over her shoulder at Ryan, Bilal and Chris. They're sniggering and poking each other, glancing at Savannah. They don't exactly look over-heated. Then she takes in my clean-jean ensemble. 'Not hot enough to try it herself, I see.'

I defend myself, guilt choking me. 'I'm – er – not interested in anyone ...'

'I'm glad.' Sal switches her attention back to Savannah. 'If we had one more Goth on board, we'd reach critical mass and implode into a black hole.'

Savannah's red-rimmed eyes spark with worry. 'Do I look silly?'

'Don't worry,' Sally comforts her. 'It's good to see you trying something ...' She fumbles for words '... new.'

Bilal hoots with laughter while Ryan turns away.

Marcus isn't laughing. He's staring at Savannah, his eyes soft. My guilt eases a little. Once again Marcus has proved he's the best boy for Savannah. If only she'd realize it.

But she's sunk into a seat and is slouching against the window. 'Oh God,' she whines as I sit next to her. 'What have I done? I can't believe I agreed to wear this.' She fixes me with an earnest look that nearly kills me. 'Are you sure Cindy's survey said *emo*?'

'Definitely.' I try to ignore the snickering at the back of the bus and focus on the fact I'm saving Savannah from heartbreak. She insists on walking into the lion's den – I'm just making sure she looks more like a cabbage than a honey-glazed ham. I sit back in my seat and persuade myself it's going to be a great evening. LJ will snub Savannah and Marcus – sweet, sweet Marcus – will be there to mop up the tears. They'll be dating within a week and living happily ever after by Easter.

We get off near the nightclub. As we reach the door, Savannah starts acting like a shrunken violet, hunching inside her flapping black coat. She shows her ticket and slinks past the doorman.

I follow, sliding my arm through hers. 'You look great, Sav,' I tell her. 'LJ is going to go nuts for you.'

'Yeah, right,' she mutters bitterly.

The club is packed. Familiar faces from school dot the crowd. On the stage at the far end of the room, Sam is fiddling with a microphone, adjusting the height. I wonder if he's nervous. This must be his biggest gig yet.

'Hi, Savannah.' A familiar American twang plucks my ear.

LJ steps from the crowd, his entourage filtering out after him.

Savannah looks ready to die. Her gaze is darting everywhere. She looks like she's trying to escape her body.

'I *love* the look.' LJ traces a finger through the air in front of her. 'Emo. Nice. And you pull it off great.' His entourage start nodding and murmuring.

I make silent goldfish noises. I'm stunned.

Savannah scrapes her chin off the floor and rolls her shoulders back. 'It was just the mood I was in,' she says casually.

'My last photo shoot was all about Goth,' LJ runs an admiring hand down Savannah's ragged collar. 'It's totally cutting edge and cool like you wouldn't believe. Black is the new black.'

Despair swamps me. I've messed up *again*!

I feel my mobile vibrate. I slide it out of my pocket. It's Will.

FOUND ANYTHING YET?

My thumb hovers over the buttons. Should I reply, ignore, or tell him I'm on the case?

If in doubt, do nothing.

As I drop the phone back into my pocket, Sam appears.

'I thought it was you.' He's grinning at me. Then he spots Savannah. 'Whoa.' He steps back. 'What's with the undead look?'

I give him my *Shh!* face, but luckily Savannah hasn't heard. She's too busy watching LJ melt back into the crowd.

'Join us,' LJ calls over his shoulder to her. She dives after him like a mermaid on a mission.

Sam scratches his head. 'Are you going too?'

Suddenly I'm torn. I want to follow Savannah to stop her throwing herself at LJ. But I need to ask Sam if he can show me backstage.

My phone vibrates again. It's Will.

SO?

I switch it off. 'Sam.' I stare at his shoes. 'I was wondering . . .'

'Yeah?'

'Would it be possible to maybe look around backstage?'

'Backstage?' He's wearing a quizzical look.

'It's just that I *love* backstage.' My mouth breaks into a gallop. 'I always have. Since I was a kid. Ballet performances. Pantos. I can't get enough of the whole greasepaint and sawdust vibe.'

Sam frowns. 'It's not exactly the London Palladium,'

he warns me. 'It's more mic stands and speaker cables than greasepaint and sawdust.'

'That's *even more* exciting!' I enthuse wildly. 'I've always wanted to know how these places work. I mean, all the glamour and glitter on the outside. I bet it's not so sparkly back there. Unless you've got a room full of glitter balls and a spare disco floor. Wow, wouldn't that be good? Your own disco floor. I would *love* to see that. It would be totally cool. And I promised Treacle I'd—'

'Come on then.' He holds out a hand and leads me into the crowd.

Sam guides me through a heavy door beside the stage. Cold air washes over me. After the dark and heat of the dance floor, the bright, chilly world of backstage leaves me blinking. A cluttered hallway splits and stretches away under strips of fluorescent light.

'Hey, Alex!' Sam waves at a T-shirted boy who's ambling along one of the breezeblock corridors. Tugging my hand, Sam hurries to catch up. I jump over cables and dodge mic stands till we skid to a halt beside Alex.

Alex is more hair than boy. When he nods a hello I catch a glimpse of a boney face through the tousled shrubbery.

'Hi.' I wave like a robot, not sure what to say.

Another grungy boy slides out of a doorway.

'Meet Gemma.' Sam says, beckoning Grunge Number Two closer. 'Gemma, this is Pete.'

Pete grabs my hand. 'Hi, Gemma.' He shakes it fiercely. His fingers are sweaty. I'm glad when he lets go.

'What do you play?' I ask. I think, *Will he notice if I wipe my hand dry on my jeans?*

'Bass.'

'Great.' I slide my hand into my back pocket and let the denim soak up Pete's sweat.

When another grunge-Bob flared-pants appears in the doorway, I slide my other hand into my other back pocket. This boy looks like he might leave more than sweat smears.

'This is Joel Kenyon, but we call him Kenny.' Sam slaps the grubby-looking boy on the back.

Kenny flops forward, then back, like a knitted toy. Then he grunts and wanders back through the doorway.

'He's not exactly a people person,' Sam explains.

Pete watches Kenny go. 'He's a great drummer though,' he adds.

Sam looks at me eagerly. 'What do you think?'

'Of Kenny?'

'Of backstage.'

I gaze around the antiseptic corridor, trying to look impressed.

'Gemma loves behind-the-scenes stuff,' Sam explains to Pete and Alex.

I shift my feet. 'Y-yeah. This is, like, where it all happens.'

Pete grins. 'We're kind of more focused on the on-stage side of things.'

'I guess.' I peer along the corridor, glimpsing some steps. 'Where does that go?'

'The stage.' Pete says looking at his watch. 'We're on in ten minutes.' He heads for the doorway. 'I'd better go and tune up.'

'Is that the dressing room?' I point to the door Kenny and Pete disappeared through.

'Yeah,' Sam steers me toward it. 'Do you want to see it?'

I'm more interested in Dave Wiggins's office but I can't tell Sam that. 'Actually, I was wondering if there was a loo round here.'

'Sure.' Sam points down the corridor, towards a fire door. 'Go through there and turn right.'

'Thanks.' I hurry away. Nerves flutter in my stomach. What if I get caught snooping? Where's Scooby Doo when you need him?

I push through the fire door, unnerved by the silence as it swings shut behind me. It's like diving underwater. I feel suddenly deaf. Then I hear a voice. It's gruff and sounds angry.

Tiptoeing along the corridor, I reach a corner and peer round. There's a door marked 'Toilet' to my right. I creep past it and head for the voice. My heart is beating so hard I can feel it in my throat. I pass an emergency exit; the door's half open, a cold breeze funnelling in from outside. A fluorescent strip hums above my head. Boxes are stacked against the walls here, leaving a narrow space down the middle of the corridor. I head along the passageway, my hand on the phone in my pocket. My palms are sweating Pete-like as the voice gets louder. I stop and peek round a mountain of boxes. Beyond it, a door is half open. Behind the door, the gruff voice is barking.

'I don't want excuses!'

Is it Dave Wiggins? I lean close and peer through the gap between the hinges. A shadowy shape moves behind a desk. This must be his office!

'The delivery was meant to be here last night!'

Dave's snarl is answered by the tinny crackle of a phone voice.

'We made a deal!' Dave snarls. 'I want those drugs!'

Drugs! Adrenaline's pumping through me like I've been stabbed with an epi-pen.

Dave's roaring down the phone. 'I've got customers lining up and they're not the sort of people who like to be kept waiting.'

I pull my phone from my pocket. I've got to record this. I quickly fumble for the memo function and hit record.

Bang!

A door slams behind me.

I turn round, heart exploding. The emergency exit is shut. The wind must have slammed it. The echoing sound seems to shake the walls.

I feel suddenly exposed. The fire door is miles behind

me. I hear footsteps crossing Dave Wiggins's office. Panicking, I step backward. Boxes tumble behind me as I stumble into them. I drop my phone and it skids, clattering, across the floor. The office door swings open. Dave Wiggins is towering over me. Six foot tall, flashing with gold rings and medallions, he looks like a gorilla. Dark hair sprouts from his orange-tanned chest and his face is thick-jawed and half shaven and topped by a wig that looks like it's been lifted by CarpetWorld.

'What are you doing here?' he yells at me.

It's worse than being shredded by a teacher.

Terror swamps me.

Teachers aren't allowed to murder you and stow your body in the back of their Mercedes. Even if they want to.

I dive after my phone, snatch it off the floor and back away. This time I avoid the boxes. 'S-sorry,' I gibber. 'I was looking for the loo. I was with the band and they said it was d-down here.'

'Is that right?' Wiggins stamps after me, eyes narrow. 'You passed the bog about ten metres back.'

I'm reversing like crazy.

'It's got "Toilet" written on the door. Not 'ard to spot.' He's still coming at me, balling his fists. 'Or are you too dumb to read?'

'Oh.' I glance behind me. 'I didn't see it.'

'But you managed to find my office.' His voice is rich with menace.

'W-was that your office?' I stammer. 'I'm sorry. I didn't mean to disturb you.'

I hear a sucking noise as the fire door opens behind me.

'Gemma?'

Relief floods me as I hear Sam's voice.

'Did you find the loo?'

Wiggins halts. He stares at me as I back towards Sam.

'Are you OK?' Sam looks worried. 'Did you get lost?'

'Yeah.' I push through the fire door, relieved to hear the faint hubbub of the nightclub in the distance. Wiggins is watching me with a frown. I shiver.

'Cold?' Sam asks.

'It's a bit chilly back here.' I feel sick. 'I'd better go out front and see if I can find Savannah.'

'There you are!' Savannah fights her way out of the crowd and stops beside me.

I need to text Will.

'Where have you been?' Savannah's leaning toward me, holding a plastic cup full of juice.

'Sam was showing me backstage.'

She raises her eyebrows. '*Really?*'

'I was interested, that's all.'

'I didn't realize.'

'Realize what?' We seem to be having different conversations.

'You and Sam.'

I'm bristling with irritation, desperate to tell Will what I've found out. 'There's nothing between me and Sam,' I snap. 'He likes Cindy. I just wanted to see what it was like backstage.'

Savannah backs off. 'Whatever.' She's taken off the huge black coat and is somehow making the emo vibe work. The tight black dress looks kind of cool and the dark lipstick is wickedly vampish under the disco lights.

'Do you want a Coke or something? LJ's made friends with the guy behind the bar. He can get anything you want.'

'A Coke would be great.' I want to distract her so I can text Will. 'Can you get me one?'

Music explodes from the stage. Sam's hanging off the mic while his band rev up behind him.

'It's started!' Savannah twitches like an excited cat. 'I'd better get back to the others. Come with me.'

I guess 'the others' are LJ and his gang.

'In a minute,' I promise. 'I told Mum I'd phone – let her know we got here all right.'

'OK.' Savannah fights her way into the crush that's massing around the stage. Her drink is slopping down her arm as she holds it above her head. 'Don't be long.' I can hardly hear her over the pounding of Sam's band. As soon as she's gone, I slide over to the wall and text Will.

Found something.

I wait for a reply, heart racing as I stare at my phone. Nothing.

I head for the foyer. Perhaps the signal's too weak here.

The foyer's cool and quiet. I check my signal. It's strong. *Come on, Will!*

I can't wait. I scroll through my contacts and dial his number.

Engaged.

What's he doing on the phone? Perhaps there's a chat-line where you get to insult Year Nines for ten pence a minute. I reckon Will would be willing to pay; he seems to enjoy it so much. I pace up and down till the bouncer on the door starts eyeing me suspiciously.

Savannah bursts out through a door, surfing a guitar riff. 'Sam's band are great!' she shouts.

The bouncer glares at her. She's talking in her loud-music voice. In the quiet of the foyer she sounds demented.

'Sorry.' She tones it down. 'Wasn't it sweet of Sam to dedicate a song to you?'

'He did?' I blink at her.

'Yes.' She glances round the glossy walls of the foyer. 'What are you doing out here anyway?'

'Phone.' I point to my mobile, trying not to give anything away. As I do, it rings, lighting up with Will's name.

Savannah eyes me suspiciously. 'What are you up to?'

'Webzine business,' I tell her vaguely.

'Now?'

I hit the answer button. 'Hi, Will.' I cover the mouthpiece. 'Go back and watch the gig,' I tell Savannah. 'In case Sam does a song for you too.'

Savannah's eyes light up. 'That would impress LJ.' She races through the door, swallowed by the music, and I'm free to talk to Will.

'Gemma?' He's yelling down the line at me. 'Are you there? What's happened?'

'Hi, Will.'

'So? What's the story? What did you find?' He's firing questions, Nazi-style, as if I don't want to tell him.

I head for a corner, as far from the bouncers as I can get, and whisper into the mouthpiece. 'I heard him say something about *drugs*.'

'Drugs!' Will sounds like I just told him he'd won the lottery *and* a lifetime's supply of leather jackets.

'I think he's dealing out of the club.' I glance furtively at the bouncer then look away before he thinks I've got a crush on him.

'I'll be there in ten minutes,' Will says. 'Meet me outside.'

Ten minutes? Is he borrowing Cindy's broomstick?

I hang up and plunge back into the heaving gloom of the club.

Explaining to Savannah that I have to go home is easier than I imagine. She's so busy watching LJ I could tell her anything: that I'm having Mr Harris's lovechild; that Treacle's head exploded over dinner and Mr and Mrs Simpson want help scraping her brains off the wallpaper. Instead, I tell her Mum's sick and needs me to look after Ben.

She just nods and smiles. 'OK.'

'So I'll see you Monday,' I shout through the screeching solo which Alex is torturing from his guitar.

'Monday, yes.' Savannah says distractedly as she moves nearer to LJ. She's been closing in on him since I started talking. You could toast sandwiches in the smouldering gap between them. I'm glad I'm leaving so I don't have to watch them flirting with each other.

Outside, it's deliciously cold. I wander up and down the empty pavement, staying in the circle of light beaming down from the streetlamp. The wind's fierce but it's not raining. I can't wait to share my discovery with Will. I check my watch, then check the sky for incoming broomsticks. As I do, a car pulls up a few metres away. Will slides out of the passenger door like a snake escaping from its tank. He slams the door shut and thumps the roof. The car speeds away. As it passes, I glimpse a middle-aged woman at the wheel.

'Was that your mum?' I ask Will as he strides toward me. It never occurred to me that Will had a mother. I'd assumed he'd sprung fully-formed and leather-jacketed from the head of Zeus, like that Greek god Mrs Dalton bangs on about. It's sweet to think he's got a mum; I picture her in an apron, serving Will a comforting bowl of soup.

'None of your business!'

My warm feeling chills as Will snarls at me.

I shrink into my jacket. 'I just wondered.'

'I didn't come here to share family secrets,' he growls. 'What did you find out?'

'Wiggins is expecting a delivery of drugs.'

'I heard that,' Will snaps. 'Give me the who-what-where-when-and-why.' He reels off the five Ws like a seasoned reporter.

I start from the very beginning. 'I found his office and listened at the door.' I glance back at the club, half nervous, half excited. 'He was on the phone to someone.'

'Did you get a name?' Will pulls a notepad from his pocket and flips it open.

I shake my head. 'He just said the delivery was meant to be last night and he wanted the drugs.'

Will scribbles something on his pad, talking as he writes. 'Did he say which sort? Weed? Coke? Heroin?'

I shake my head 'I just heard *drugs*.'

Will's nodding. 'Anything else?'

'He sounded pretty desperate,' I tell him. 'He said "I've got customers in line and they're not the sort of people who like to be kept waiting".'

Will slaps his pad shut. 'Nice job.'

I wait for the follow-up comment. The sharp remark that will cut me off at the knees. It doesn't come.

'We've really got something to go on now.' Will's running his hand though his hair. Nervous energy's sparking from him like static. 'I'll get us tickets for next week's gig. We can come back together and do some more digging.'

Together! He's really taking me seriously. I squash back my joy and focus on the story. 'Shouldn't we stake the place out?' I ask. 'That delivery might be tonight.'

Will frowns. 'Too dangerous.' He shakes his head. 'This could be big, but we need to tread carefully.'

We take the same bus home. I'm kind of glad. Buses after dark aren't my favourite thing.

'Cindy's dying to know what the story's about,' I tell him as we perch next to the luggage rack and watch the streetlamps flash by.

'You didn't tell her, did you?' He slides his feet restlessly over the filthy floor.

'Nope.'

'Good.'

'Is she as tough in class as she is in editorial meetings?' I want to get a Year-Ten view of the Ice Queen.

'A good editor needs to be tough.'

I'm surprised to hear him defend her. I decide to shut up. A good bitching session takes two, and he's clearly not playing. My phone bleeps. It's a text from Treacle.

GREAT NIGHT. JEFF'S PARENTS GREAT. JEFF SUPER-SWEET. THANX FOR SUPPORT. XXX

I smile. When Treacle's happy, I'm happy. Especially when I've just busted a drug ring wide open too. My first story and I've hit the jackpot. My name is going to be famous once this reaches the presses. I slide into a daydream. An eager reporter from the local paper is doorstepping me.

'When did you first discover Wiggins was dealing heroin?' His notepad is open.

Before I can answer, a man in a slick, grey suit pushes past and offers me his card. 'Gemma Stone?'

I nod.

'Great story.' He takes my hand and shakes it. 'Our paper needs reporters like you. Young blood. In touch with the street.'

The scene in my head cuts to a London news office. Monitors hum, keyboards rattle, reporters dart between cluttered cubicles.

'Stone!' The chief news editor calls me from his office. 'Get in here.'

I hurry in and sit down as my boss paces. 'I just got the call,' he tells me. 'Your piece on Britain's biggest drug cartel has been nominated for Top Story at the International News Awards.' He stops and gazes at me in wonder. 'I can't believe you're only fifteen. You'll be the youngest award winner ever.'

'*If* I win,' I caution him.

'You'll win, Stone,' he tells me. 'You'll win.'

12

'Catch!' Dad lobs the salt pot at me. It flies across the dining table and I catch it like a pro.

It's Sunday dinner and Dad's trying to blow away the Monday morning blues that are just starting to settle over the house like a fog.

'Philip Stone!' Mum scolds Dad like he's one of the kids. 'What kind of example are you setting?'

It's too late. Ben's a quick learner. He's already snatched up the pepper pot and thrown it at Dad.

Dad flings out a hand and catches it clumsily. Pepper puffs from the top, straight up his nose. His eyes goggle. His nose twitches and he explodes.

The sneezing fit lasts a full five minutes. Dad's nose is machine-gunning. It blasts him twice round the dining table.

Ben drops to the floor, helpless with laughter, and rolls there howling while I hang off my chair, clutching my sides in a fit of giggles.

Mum flaps after Dad, offering tissues and snatching

ornaments from his path. 'Are you OK, honey?' she gasps each time he comes up for air.

At last Dad staggers against a wall and collapses dramatically. 'I'm dying,' he splutters, before giving himself up to another gigantic sneeze.

Ben crawls under the table and out the other side, then flops down beside Dad. 'You're the funniest Dad in the world.'

Dad wraps an arm around Ben, eyes streaming. 'Thanks, Pepper-Boy.' He plants a kiss on Ben's head then hauls himself and Ben up.

We settle back down to dinner.

'How's school, Gem?' Mum takes advantage of the lull to slide in her favourite question.

'Fine.' I know she wants more detail, but there isn't enough time to explain the whole geopolitical situation at Green Park High and, without a firm grasp of the basics, she'd make no sense of current events in my educational universe.

'How's Treacle?' Mum presses.

'Fine.' I'll save the Jeff-parents-meeting exposé till I've got more time.

'Savannah?' Mum should be a quiz-show host. 'She was looking a little peaky on Friday.' She must have glimpsed Sav's emo-transformation as we headed up the driveway.

'She's fine.' I make a mental note to bring Mum up to

speed on the various plot points in my life. But right now I want to hoover up my sausage and mash and finish Jessica Jupiter's horoscopes. It's deadline day tomorrow and, with the rest of the editorial team hogging keyboards, I can't guarantee computer access at the webzine HQ.

'Don't you want pudding?' Mum asks as I clatter my knife and fork together on my plate and push back my chair. 'It's cheesecake.'

Cheesecake! I hesitate. Mum makes kick-ass cheesecake. 'Can I have it later?' I ask. 'When I've finished my homework?'

The H-word works wonders and Mum beams. 'Of course, pet. I'll save you some.'

It's not like me to turn down Mum's cheesecake, but words are rattling round my head and I want to get them on to my hard disk before they escape.

I head for my room and settle down on my beanbag with my battered old laptop.

<u>Libra</u>

I start with my own star sign. Since my exciting scoop at Sounds, dreams about my brilliant career have been filling my head. Perhaps, if I put them into my horoscope they might come true.

Dear, level-headed Libra. A lucky break on the work front might have tipped the scales in your favour. After proving your true worth this week, you'll be able to trade in your dull,

113

dusty life for one that's as star-filled and fabulous as mine. You lucky, lucky Star-ling.

Once I've etched my future in stone – or at least tapped it into pixels – I move on to Marcus.

I remember him moon-eyed on the bus, watching Sav, and wonder how he spent the rest of the evening. Probably wallflowering while Savannah flitted round LJ like a butterfly in a hothouse.

Sagittarius

I finally managed to find his birthday without pasting him all over my Facebook status.

Take heart, Star-ling, all is not lost. Though it may seem hopeless, the apple of your eye is still on the tree. Stay close by and it may still drop into your lap. And if you want first bite, don't do a Newton and worry about the gravity of the situation, sink your teeth in and enjoy the sweetness.

Sam's next. He deserves a mention. After all it was Sam who got me into the gig and backstage for my scoop.

Capricorn

Last week you outshone the stars. The most naturally gifted of all the signs, you're like a rocket headed for the moon. Last week's step will be a giant leap before you know it. Don't forget to pack a flag. You're going to need something to plant when you get there.

I pick up my phone and scroll though my texts, re-reading the sweet one from Sam, sent late Friday night.

You OK?

He'd asked Savannah for my number when he couldn't find me after the gig.

Sam's such a nice guy. I add a line to his horoscope.

Enjoy your success. You deserve it. You're the most caring sign in the zodiac.

The doorbell rings and I hear Mum chatting. Treacle's voice drifts up from the hall. She's come for our usual pre-Monday pep-talk. Mum will be giving her a light grilling, hoping to extract more info than she got from me at dinner. I wonder whether to rescue her but decide she can handle it. She's like Mum's other daughter and I want a few minutes extra to write Sav's horoscope. It's an easy one. I've decided to cut trying to be subtle. This time I don't want her to misunderstand Jessica's warning. And I definitely don't want her quizzing me about Jessica again.

<u>Pisces</u>

Hey, fish-face! Prick up your gills and listen. For a guppy you have an awfully sweet tooth. But stop gorging yourself on imported cheesecake. You'll make yourself sick. If you see a label marked USA, back away and look for something home-grown.

I hear Treacle on the stairs. She's clattering.

'Your Mum asked me to bring these up.' She pushes my door open with a foot. She's carrying two plates with cheesecake. She passes me one and flumps on to my bed.

She's already forked in a mouthful by the time she starts speaking. It's not pretty to watch but when you're a best friend you have to take the rough with the smooth.

'It wuz brulliunt,' she tells me, through the chewed-up cake.

I wait for her to swallow. 'The dinner with Jeff's Olds?'

She nods and forks another lump of cheesecake from the slice. Before she can load it into her mouth, I slap my plate on to the desk and zip across the room.

I land next to her and hold down her fork. 'Give me the cake-free version.'

'OK.' She pushes her plate into my hands and leaps to her feet. 'I arrive, right? And it's all "Hello, Mrs Simpson. Hello, Mr Simpson. Can I take your coat?" That's my coat, not theirs – they weren't wearing coats. And Jeff's hopping from one foot to another behind them, with this terrified look like they're performing open-heart surgery on the cat.'

'He's got a cat?'

'No.' She waves away the question. 'Anyway, we get the hellos done, then they ask if I want to sit down and I say, "what, here?" And I'm looking round the hall wondering if we're going to sit on the stairs and chat, which of course is really stupid but I'm so nervous my brain's not fully functioning, but Mrs S is lovely and suggests we use the sitting room and I'm expecting the third degree, but they just disappear into the kitchen and leave me and Jeff on our own. So then I get paranoid and wonder if they've gone to talk about me but Jeff says they're cooking this big tea and I get more nervous in case I can't eat or they're roasting a giraffe or something equally gross and he says not to worry it's just chicken.'

I lean on a pillow and make myself comfortable, it seems like this is going to be a long story.

Treacle gets up and starts pacing. 'I'm just starting to unwind when Mr S – Trevor – comes in and he's wearing an apron and he asks if I want juice and I say yes.'

I take a mouthful of Treacle's cheesecake. I'm clearly going to need sustenance. She's in full flow.

'So we drink juice and I'm feeling really relaxed now because the house is, like, totally normal with piles of newspapers and books like they've sort of tidied up but not gone mad. And then Mrs S comes out and perches on the arm of the sofa and starts talking about how pleased she is to meet me and how she hopes I like garlic because Trevor – Mr S – goes a bit nuts with it. And I say, "At least he's not a vampire," and Mrs S laughs.' Treacle stops and stares at me. 'She actually *laughed*, Gem, and then she said, "I've always preferred werewolves". And I agreed with her because werewolves are much cooler than vampires. I mean vampires are so puny. They're allergic to practically everything – sun, Bibles, crosses, garlic. It's amazing any of them ever make a kill. I mean if a normal human was allergic to that much stuff they'd have to live in a bubble with the lights out.'

I swallow another mouthful of cheesecake. 'Did you share all this with Mrs S?'

'Jane,' Treacle corrects me. 'I'm meant to call her Jane.'

'She sounds nice.'

'She is!' Treacle sounds amazed. 'Because I *did* share all that stuff about vampires because I couldn't shut up. I was so nervous I couldn't stop talking.'

I grin. I know the feeling well.

'But she loved it and we had this big discussion about vampires and how werewolves would totally rule them and then Trevor came in and said dinner was ready.'

'Garlic chicken?'

'How did you guess?'

'And you offered to help?'

'Are you psychic or something?'

'I write horoscopes, don't forget,' I remind her. 'I'm in touch with a higher plane. I can see everything.'

Treacle flicks her hair back. 'You're just guessing.'

'Yep.' I shovel in another piece of Treacle's cheese-cake. 'What happened next?'

'I got through dinner without choking on a bone or spilling my juice and then—'

'Did they interrogate you?'

'Oh, yeah, kind of.' Treacle's casual. 'But it was OK because they were really interested. Like I was a *real* person, not just their son's girlfriend.'

'Jeff is lucky to have you,' I comment.

'That's what Jane said!' Treacle grabs the plate of cheesecake I left by my laptop and sits beside me. 'She said she's glad he's interested in something apart from football for a change.'

'So it went well?'

Treacle smiles a wide smile. 'I think they actually like me.'

I nudge her. 'Of course they do! What's not to like?'

Treacle digs into my cheesecake. 'They didn't even seem cross when I sat on Mr Woofy.'

I blink. 'Mr Woofy?'

'Their chameleon.'

I gulp. 'Chameleon?'

'I didn't sit down hard,' Treacle explains. 'I kind of spotted him just as I was about to land.'

'So you avoided splatting their pet chameleon?'

'Yeah.' Treacle sounds relieved. 'And they didn't mind the screaming at all.'

'Screaming?'

Treacle shoots me a serious look. 'Have *you* ever nearly sat on a chameleon?'

I shake my head.

'Then don't judge.' Treacle sniffs. 'It's more surprising

than you'd imagine. Frankly I think anyone would've screamed.'

'So apart from nearly killing their pet and the screaming, the evening went well?'

'Jeff said I was brilliant.' Treacle fills her mouth with more cake. 'And they said I was welcome any time.'

I feel really proud. Treacle must have charmed Jeff's parents if they forgave a near murder *and* a screaming session.

Treacle scoffs down the last of the biscuity base. 'So how was Sounds?'

'It was OK.' I take her plate and stack it on mine. I'm dying to tell her about my scoop but I'm scared of jeopardizing the investigation.

'Were Sam's band good?'

I can't tell her I missed most of the set. 'Yeah. Savannah loved them.'

As I mention Savannah, I hear a familiar voice at the bottom of the stairs.

'Thanks, Sarah. I'll try it, I promise.'

I jerk up. 'Is that Savannah?'

Treacle tucks her hair behind her ear. 'You *must* be psychic, Gem,' she says as footsteps patter up the stairs and Savannah swings in through my bedroom. 'You can summon demons.'

Savannah's still kitted out like the creature from the black lagoon. She peers at us from gruesome purple- and black-rimmed eyes. 'Oh, ha-ha,' she huffs, collapsing on to my bed. 'I've been dressing like an emo all weekend and he's not even called me.'

Treacle looks puzzled.

'LJ,' I explain. 'He really liked Sav's emo-look.'

'He *liked* it?' Treacle blurts.

I cover her blunder. 'Yes, because it's the hottest look, remember?' Savannah's not meant to know we wanted him to hate it.

Savannah sniffs. 'But not hot enough to make him ask me out.'

Phew! When I left Sounds I thought Savannah had conquered Mount LJ, but clearly his admiration went no further than a smile.

Savannah's splayed on the duvet like a corpse. 'He didn't even ask for my number.' Her face crumples. 'He left with his arm around Bethany.'

Her sob slices my heart. Me and Treacle are beside her instantly, arms round her.

'What am I doing wrong?' Tears well in her eyes. Savannah's so used to slaying every man she sees, the shock must be terrible. Savannah breaks loose and starts pacing the floor. 'What's wrong with me? First Josh chooses Chelsea and now LJ goes for Bethany Richards!' She turns, her eyes earnest. 'Have I turned ...?' Her breath comes in short panicky gasps. 'Have I gone ...?' She swallows. 'Ugly?'

A snort of laughter bursts from Treacle.

I grab a pillow and slap it over her. 'Treacle!' I use my stern voice. 'This is serious.' But I understand Treacle's amusement. Savannah Smith saying she's ugly is like Einstein whining that he's dumb. But Savannah's really heartbroken and it's no laughing matter.

Savannah slumps to the floor, her eyeliner running. She squats like a wounded crow, her black tattered dress billowing round her. I can hardly believe my eyes. This tragic heartbreak victim, flailing hopelessly on my bedroom floor, used to be the Queen of Cool.

Suddenly I miss the old Savannah.

It's time for some drastic action.

Double Maths on a Monday afternoon. What kind of sicko invented that? By the time the bell goes, my head's drowning in numbers.

Treacle starts packing her book bag beside me. 'You've got the webzine meeting, right?'

I nod. 'Are you going to wait for Jeff?'

'And you.' She ties her shiny black hair into a ponytail. 'I'm gonna practise penalties on the field. Then we can all get the bus home together.' She skims me a high-five and heads for the door.

I grab my books and my bag and slide through the going-home crowds flooding the halls. I'm swimming against the tide and, by the time I reach webzine HQ, I'm crushed and tousled. I smooth my hair, relieved that my curls are still soft for a change, and head into the storeroom.

I'm expecting the room to be crammed after last Monday, when the Year Ten webziners took their study period here. So I'm surprised to find Sam's the only one in the room. He's one-finger typing on his usual PC.

'Where is everyone?' I ask. I want to speak to Will and find out if he's got any more news on Dave Wiggins.

Sam stops poking his keyboard. 'They're robbing the tuck shop.'

I wonder about suggesting to Will that we dig through business directories on the web, to see if we can trace any involvement by Wiggins in other companies.

When I don't answer him, Sam says, 'I was kidding – about the tuck shop. There's a career talk in the library.' He looks at his watch. 'They'll be here in a minute.'

'Didn't you want to go to the career talk?'

Sam leans back on his chair. 'I know what career I want.'

'Rock star?'

'Environmental lawyer.'

My eyebrows shoot up.

Sam grins. 'We all need a plan B.'

Do we? I can't imagine working as anything other than a journalist. It's my plan A *and* B.

'So, you left the gig on Friday early?' Sam's casual question takes me by surprise. The gig's the last thing on my mind.

The door swings wide and Will strides in.

Sam's gaze stays on me. 'I was worried our music might have scared you away.'

Will dumps his bag on his desk. 'She had to meet me.' He swings into his chair and puts his feet on the desk.

Sam splutters. '*You?*'

Will grins at him. 'Can I help it if I'm irresistible?'

I roll my eyes. But I can't set him straight without giving away our scoop.

Sam's narrowed his gaze. 'I thought Gemma had more taste.'

'Clearly not.' Will reaches in his pocket and pulls out two blue tickets. 'Look, Gemma. I got us into next week's gig.' He waves them at me.

'Fantastic!' I'm thrilled. Working together in the club, Will and I must be able to track down some hard evidence on Dave Wiggins.

Sam turns to Will. 'You're going to the gig with Gemma?'

I stare at Sam. 'So?' He's the last person I expect to be shocked at a Year Nine and Year Ten being seen out together, and I have to admit that I'm a little hurt by his reaction.

Will laughs. 'Don't worry, Sam. I'll take care of her.'

Sam snorts. 'You're all heart, Will.'

He gets up and start zipping his backpack.

'Aren't you staying for the meeting?' I'm confused.

Sam doesn't look up. 'Why bother? I've emailed Cindy my article and next week's piece is sorted.'

'Don't go, Sam.' Cindy wafts into the room in a cloud of perfume. Barbara drifts in after her.

'I've got to meet someone,' Sam growls.

'This is a team meeting,' Cindy pleads. 'And you're an important part of the team.' She rests her delicate fingers on his arm. 'Stay,' she murmurs. 'Please.' Her throaty purr seems to work. He drops his bag and slumps back down into his chair.

'OK,' he mutters.

'Gemma.' Will's beckoning me. I lean in close and he whispers in my ear. 'Keep it zipped,' he warns. 'Don't give anything away to Cinders about the story.'

'Duh!' I grab a chair as Phil and Dave filter in.

Jeff follows, a football crammed into his book bag.

Cindy perches on her desk while we draw up our chairs. 'Glad you could all make it.' She flashes a smile, which lingers on Sam. 'And I was delighted to see so many articles in my inbox by lunchtime.' Her gaze pans to Will. 'Except yours, of course, Will.' Her sweet voice turns sour. 'I was *so* looking forward to the fabulous story you promised us last week.'

Will shrugs. 'Sorry, Cinders. It's still a work in progress.' He nods towards me. 'Me and Gemma still have some research to cover. I'm not turning in any facts until they're properly checked.'

Me and Gemma. I'm overheating with excitement. I'm going to be contributing something worthwhile to the webzine at last.

Cindy narrows her eyes. 'So what *are* you turning in for this week's edition then, William?'

'I've got a back-up piece on school trip fatality rates.' He scratches his nose. 'I'll dig it out and email it as soon as I get home.'

Cindy tuts like a primary-school teacher. 'It's a shame you and Gemma didn't manage to get more work done.'

Will's gaze is steady. 'We got plenty of work done.'

'I bet you did,' Sam mutters.

'But you can't hurry a good story.' Will leans back in his chair. 'Don't worry, it'll be well worth waiting for.'

Cindy purses her lips so hard, I'm scared she'll smudge her lipstick.

Barbara shoots up her hand. 'Shall I tell everyone about my new piece?'

This week I don't care what drippy trash she comes out with. I'm working on something important.

Barbara smiles. '*Helping Out with Chores: Ten Steps to a Harmonious Home.*'

Will pounces. 'Washing up for the washed-up,' he quips.

'Leave it, Will.' Sam scowls at him. 'Some of us help out at home. Not all of us are obsessed with ourselves.'

I turn in my seat, surprised. Sam's usually the peacemaker. It's not like him to start firing on his team-mates.

Cindy sweeps her lashes in Sam's direction. 'Thank you, Sam,' she says gratefully. 'It's nice to hear someone supporting their colleagues instead of critiquing.' She scans our faces. 'Anyone else want to share?'

Dave sticks up his hand. 'Me and Phil have been reviewing in-ear headphones.'

Cindy tips her head to one side. 'How interesting.'

Phil chimes in enthusiastically. 'We've got a top five and the most economical.'

'Sounds great.' Cindy turns to Jeff. 'Did you manage to cover the important school matches?'

Jeff nods. "Yes, I've got reports from the Year Ten Girls and the Year Nine Boys.'

'Good, good,' Cindy says distractedly, gazing back at Sam.

Jeff looks at me and raises his eyebrows – his code for *What is up with this girl?* I grin and nod my head in Sam's direction – my code for *She's suffering from a deadly case of smitten-kitten-itis.*

Cindy carries on gazing at Sam and actually flutters her eyelashes. I thought people only ever did that in naff novels. 'I *loved* your gig, Sam.'

She'd been there? I don't know why I'm surprised. Sam probably gave her tickets. I hadn't noticed her in the crowd. I'd been too busy worrying about Savannah and Dave Wiggins to watch out for the Ice Queen.

Cindy goes on. 'It was sweet of you to give Gemma a backstage tour.' Her mouth smiles. Her eyes don't.

She saw us?

I'm amazed she recognized me out of uniform.

'Yeah, well.' Sam stares at his boots. 'I was just trying to be nice.'

Will straightens. 'Maybe you could give her another tour this week?' he suggests. 'I could tag along. I've always been interested in what goes on behind the scenes at gigs.'

I chew nervously on a strand of hair. Sam's going to get suspicious if we both declare our backstage fetish.

'No way,' Sam tells Will. 'Having more than one punter backstage would create a health and safety issue.'

Cindy leans forward. 'Maybe *I* could be the lucky one to get the backstage tour this week?'

'Maybe.' Sam gets to his feet. 'I've got to go.' He throws his backpack over his shoulder. 'By the way, my piece is on how tough it is for a new band to break into the mainstream.' He tugs the door open. 'Perhaps I should have focused on backstage groupies.' He's out the door before anyone can say goodbye.

I figure he's joking about the groupies. He must be weirded out by everyone wanting to see his dressing room. I wish I could explain it's for the story but he'll find out soon enough.

'Can we go too?' Phil and Dave get up.

Will heaves his bag on to his lap. 'Might as well.'

Cindy doesn't put up a fight. I guess with Sam gone, she's lost interest.

'Are you coming, Gem?' Jeff's in the doorway. 'Treacle's waiting.'

Cindy holds up a hand. 'Gemma?' She's suspiciously sweet. 'Would you stay for a moment? I want a word.'

I wonder what she's up to. 'Go without me,' I tell Jeff. 'I'll catch the next bus.'

'Are you sure?' he asks.

'Yeah,' I reply.

Will's already loping toward the staircase as Jeff follows Phil and Dave out into the hallway.

Barbara lingers at the door.

'I won't be long,' Cindy tells her.

Barbara nods. 'I'll wait in the entrance hall.'

I wonder for the first time if Cindy's told her about my secret role as Jessica Jupiter. They're as tight as superglued twins and Barbara seems the kind of friend you can trust with a secret.

'Is that OK, Gemma?' Cindy asks politely.

'Sure,' I tell her. 'What's up?'

Barbara clops away down the hall and I wait for Cindy to stop the Sugar Plum Fairy act. But she doesn't.

'I just wanted to check in with you to see how everything's going,' she says. Immediately I'm suspicious, Cindy is never nice to me. 'I checked Jessica's email account today and it looks like she's still getting a lot of fan mail, so you need to keep on top of that, OK?' She glances out of the window.

'OK,' I agree. 'I'll take a look now and send some responses.'

'Great.' Something in Cindy's tone tells me she's not finished. 'So,' she begins, 'how's working with Will going?'

'Not as scary as I thought.'

'He can be a bit arrogant,' she sighs. 'I was worried about putting the two of you together.'

I'm not convinced. 'Really?'

She ignores me. 'So, it's a good story?'

'Great.' I know she's fishing. But I'm not as dumb as she thinks.

'Is it topical?'

'I guess.' I'm pleased that I manage to stay vague.

'Is it to do with school?'

'Not really,' I murmur, though I suspect that, if Wiggins is dealing drugs out of the club, some Green Park students might be buying them.

Cindy keeps probing. 'So it's more of a local issue?'

'Why don't you wait and see?' I decide to take evasive action. 'I should get on with that fan mail. I've got to look after my brother later and I've got a ton of home-work.' I switch on a PC.

Cindy doesn't argue. I watch her out of the corner of my eye while she buttons her coat. Why isn't she giving me the third degree? Conversations with Cindy usually involve bullet-dodging. But here I am, no body armour and still not taking any hits.

She needs me! The realization pops into my head. Jessica Jupiter is the only columnist on the webzine getting emails and I'm the only Jessica she's got.

Cindy heads for the door. 'I'll see you Wednesday, Gemma.'

'Bye.' I wave her out, then type in my username, my heart pounding with excitement. I'm no longer just a helpless Year Nine she can dump on. The tide is coming in and my stranded-whale career is finally lifting off the bottom.

Dear Miss Jupiter
I love your horoscopes but I'm very worried. Last
week you predicted a cat would surprise me.

(Next door's cat knocked the lid off the dustbin while
I was writing the prediction for Aquarius. Once I'd
stopped trembling from the sudden clatter outside my
bedroom window, I'd used the incident as 'inspiration'.)

I have a phobia of cats and now I'm terrified
they're lurking wherever I go. Please tell me the
exact time and place I'll be attacked by cats so I
can avoid them.
Yours truly,
Rachel Spalding

Poor Rachel! I quickly type a reply.

Star-ling, don't worry. The danger is over. If the
cat's not surprised you by now, then you're safe.

You're free as Tweety-Pie when Sylvester's at the vet's. And looking at your star chart, I can see that your future is utterly feline-free.
Kisses
Jessica

I open the next.

Jessica,
I'm a boy so I don't read horoscopes but last week you told Scorpio to wear less make-up.

(Cindy's Scorpio. Enough said.)

If I did read horoscopes that would be stupid, unless I was some sort of Goth (which I'm not), so please make your horoscopes less girly, in case a boy does decide to read them (which they won't).
Cheers,
Anonymous
jezevans145@hotmail.com

Jez Evans clearly isn't exactly a rocket scientist, but it's a fair point. I make a mental note not to let my horoscopes get so personal in future. I don't want to ignore half my readership.

Dear Anonymous,
How thoughtless of me.
Do forgive.
From now on, I promise I'll give as much advice
to boys (and Goths) as I do to our prettier read-
ers, even though you'll never read it.
Much love
Jessica

The next one is from someone called matchstick-
girl@gmail.com. I start reading, wondering what
nonsense it'll be this time.

Dear Jessica,
Thank you so much for your wonderful horoscopes. They've really helped me in the past. I
just hope you can help me now. I'm in love with
a boy called LJ.

(*Join the queue*, I think.)

I saw him at a gig on Friday and he was so nice
to me but, at the end of the evening, he left with
someone else and he hasn't spoken to me since.
My heart is breaking.
Please tell me if we're compatible or if my love is
doomed. He's a Taurus and I'm Pisces. I'm sure

we're meant to be together, but if the stars don't agree I'll know it's hopeless.
Yours desperately,
matchstickgirl

Oh, no! This isn't just any girl who's love-sick for LJ, it has to be from Savannah! Worry grabs me and pushes me back in my chair. Was I wrong to interfere? Perhaps I shouldn't have made her dress like an emo. LJ might have walked her home instead of Bethany. And Savannah would be happy instead of heartbroken.

Guilt nibbles at me as I start typing. I'm going to put things right.

Dear matchstickgirl
I have wonderful news! Pisces and Taureans are made for each other. Pursue your love. He's a lucky boy. Let nothing get in the way of this match made in heaven!
Yours fondly,
Jessica

I hit send and vow never again to make Savannah's love life unhappy. From now on I'm going to be nothing but positive and supportive of her romantic dreams. It's not up to me to decide what's best for her.

Outside the window the sky is dark. Streetlights are

flickering on. I'd better head home before Mum starts to worry.

I power down the computer and shrug on my jacket. My schoolbag's heavy with Monday-night homework. I lug it over my shoulder and flick off the storeroom light.

The corridor echoes as I head for the stairs. Classroom lights are on as the cleaners make their rounds. My shoes click-clack on the chipped stone as I run down the stairs.

The emergency exit at the bottom is held open by a heavy Hoover. The cleaners must be taking the shortcut to the bins. I slip out. I can cut past the PE block this way and leave by the back gate. It comes out right by the bus stop.

I zip my jacket up as the cold wind hits me and follow the path past the bins. As I round the corner of the PE block, I hear voices. Boys are laughing and joking in the sheltered entrance. I can't see who it is, but my journalistic curiosity takes over and I slow my pace to listen.

'No way, guys!' I recognize an American accent.

'Then why did you spend Friday night flirting with her?' a teasing voice challenges.

I peer round the corner. LJ's hanging with two Year Tens – Mark Eagles and Harry Cosenza.

'It's just fun.' LJ's leaning against the wall, one knee bent, foot pressed against the brinks. 'It's cute the way she trails around after me.'

'She is really fit,' Harry comments. 'Even dressed like an emo.'

They're talking about Savannah!

'I'd date her,' Mark adds.

'Yeah, right.' LJ's dismissive. 'Who wants to date a Year Nine? Their moms probably still decide their bedtime.'

I resist the urge to jump out and argue.

'I think you fancy her,' Harry teases LJ. 'You just won't admit it.'

'Oh, please.' LJ pulls a face. 'I'm a model, not a childminder. Why bother with a girl when I can get any *woman* I want?'

Fury rises like lava inside me. I step back, balling my fists. I'd like to punch that arrogant jerk right on the nose.

Then I remember Jessica's email.

Oh no!

I'd encouraged Savannah to try harder with LJ because I thought it would cheer her up. Now she's going to end up even more heartbroken.

Hunching my shoulders, I stride past LJ and his stupid friends. My gaze strafes the ground and I dig my hands in my pockets and vow to work doubly hard to stop Savannah mooning over LJ.

'I still can't believe it!' Savannah's clutching her smartphone to her heart while Mrs Dalton walks the aisles of the English room, dumping copies of *Romeo and Juliet* on each desk. 'We're a match made in heaven.' She shows me the email from Jessica again. 'The stars are on our side. I knew Jessica would get it right about LJ!'

I droop, dismayed. It's eighteen hours later and LJ's mocking comments are still ringing in my ears. Poor Savannah has no idea he's amused by her crush and I've just made the situation worse with my stupid advice.

Mrs Dalton stops beside our desk. 'I'm glad to hear your stars aren't crossed, Savannah.' She arches an eyebrow. 'Perhaps you'd like to read Juliet?'

'Oh no, Miss.' Savannah clutches her throat. 'I think I'm coming down with something.'

Treacle leans in from my other side. 'She's got a bad case of American fever.'

Mrs Dalton arches her other eyebrow sceptically. She's a master of facial expressions. I think she must have been a mime in a previous life. 'If you have, keep it to your-self, dear.' She marches back to the head of the class. 'Marcus?'

Marcus jerks up his head as she calls him.

'You made such a fine job of Byron's love poem in assembly, will you come and read Romeo for me?'

Bilal hoots from his desk. 'Yo, Romeo. It's time to get your love on.' He waves his arms, making gangsta fingers.

Mrs Dalton stares Bilal down. 'Have you been watching too much MTV again?'

'You know it, Miss.' Bilal grins wide.

Marcus hauls himself to his feet and walks like a condemned man to the front of the class.

Ryan catcalls from the back. 'Romeo, Romeo, wherefore art thou, Romeo?'

Chelsea glances over her shoulder at him. 'He's standing by Miss, stupid.'

Mrs Dalton sighs and hands Marcus a copy of the play. 'Page sixty-eight,' she instructs.

While Marcus is fumbling with his book, Mrs Dalton holds up another copy. 'And who will be our Juliet?'

Savannah grabs my hand and lifts it like a boxing ref declaring the winner. 'Gem would love to do it!'

I snatch my hand away, a blush running like scarlet fever over me. 'No I wouldn't.'

Mrs Dalton smiles warmly at me. 'It would be good

experience,' she encourages. 'If you can face thirty Year Nines, you can face anything.'

I glare at Savannah but she just smiles sweetly and whispers, 'This could be your chance to reel Marcus in.'

Oh my God. She still thinks that I have a crush on Marcus!

'I told you I don't like him!' I hiss.

'I know that's what you *said*, but—'

Mrs Dalton interrupts our whispered discussion. 'Come on, Gemma.'

I get up and put one foot in front of the other till I'm level with Marcus at the head of the class.

I don't look at him. I just take the book from Mrs D and flick to page sixty-eight.

'Start from the top,' Mrs Dalton orders.

I obey.

'If thou dost love, pronounce it faithfully.

Or if thou thinkest I am too quickly won,'

I'm reading Juliet's lines like a robot.

'I'll frown, and be perverse, and say thee nay,

So thou wilt woo; but else, not for the world.'

Woo? This is worse than I even imagined. I've just said 'woo' out loud. In public. I keep my eyes on the text and press on.

'In truth, fair Montague, I am too fond,

And therefore thou mayst think my havior light;

But trust me, gentleman, I'll prove more true

141

Than those that have more cunning to be strange—'

Mrs Dalton interrupts me. 'Try and give it a little warmth,' she suggests. 'After all, Juliet is *o'erwhelmed* by love.'

I don't have to worry about blushing. All the blood has rushed to my toes. I feel pale as the moon as I launch into the next lines.

'I should have been more strange, I must confess,
But that thou overheard'st, ere I was ware,
My true love passion.'

I steal a glance at Marcus. Someone's ripped off his head and stuck a beetroot in its place. His agonized gaze flashes toward mine.

Oh no.

My heart plummets.

There's a look of apology in his eyes.

He feels sorry for me! Marcus thinks I'm meaning every soppy word of the script. I screen him out. The rest of the class snicker and whisper. I focus on getting through the next few lines.

'Therefore pardon me,
And not impute this yielding to light love,
Which the dark night hath so discovered.'

I make it to the end of my speech and cling to my book as Marcus clears his throat and starts reading from his text.

'Lady, by yonder blessed moon I vow,

That tips with silver all these fruit-tree tops.'
I take over.
'O, swear not by the moon, th' inconstant moon,
That monthly changes in her circle orb,
Lest that thy love prove likewise variable.'
Bilal sticks up his hand. 'Does anyone know what they're talking about?'

Mrs Dalton steps forward. 'Good question, Bilal.' She scans the class. 'Does anybody know what they're saying?'

A bemused murmur ripples through the class. Then Treacle sticks up her hand. 'You can't trust the moon?'

Ryan laughs. 'Maybe they're werewolves.'

'Or vampires,' Sally adds. 'Go on, Romeo,' she calls to Marcus. 'Sink your teeth into Gemma's neck. It might make it a bit more interesting.'

Marcus shifts beside me.

I died about four minutes ago, so I don't care.

'What do you think it's about, Gemma?' Mrs Dalton's question catches me by surprise. I glance back over the lines, relieved to engage my brain in something other than death by humiliation.

'I guess Juliet's saying that she wants Romeo to tell her he loves her, but she's worried she's put him off by being too honest about the way she feels. She's wondering if she should have played more mind-games with him before saying how she felt, but there wasn't time for that because when she said she loved him she thought no one was listening . . .'

My rambling explanation stumbles to a halt.

Bilal pipes up. 'It's a bit like she's accidentally declared her love in her Facebook status.'

The class roars with laughter.

'And now she's hoping he'll declare it back.' Chelsea pushes home the point.

'Now, now, class.' Mrs Dalton calms the laughter. She looks puzzled and delighted by the sudden enthusiasm. 'You've got it exactly but we need to keep the volume down. There are other classes trying to work.'

Marcus is staring at me like a celebrity confronting a stalker.

Chelsea's on a roll. 'Maybe if Juliet hadn't squawked like a lovesick parrot, Romeo wouldn't have died at the end.'

Mrs Dalton is pacing now, eyes bright. 'But would that have been a better ending?'

'It would've been better for Romeo,' Ryan calls.

'But was Shakespeare writing the play for Romeo?' Mrs Dalton presses.

I hand Mrs Dalton the book and head back to my chair.

'Thanks, Gemma.' Mrs Dalton hardly notices as she launches into her post-match analysis.

I slide down low in my seat.

Marcus does the same.

Savanna whispers in my ear. 'You should go for him, Gemma.' She nods toward Marcus. 'Did you hear how he was reading Romeo's part? I reckon he's a real romantic.'

'But *I'm not interested in him*,' I mutter.

'Then why were you blushing so much?' Savannah gives me doe-eyes and I silently wish I had a hunting rifle.

'Marcus is a real sweetie.' Savannah sighs.

My frustration ebbs as I hear wistfulness in her voice. Perhaps there's still a chance to re-focus Savannah's gaze on to Marcus. She clearly thinks he's Definitely Dateable.

Savannah doodles a love-heart on her jotter. 'I bet LJ's a sweetie when you get to know him.' My spark of hope sputters and dies. 'Hearing Romeo and Juliet being all gooey has inspired me.' Savannah's embellishing her doodle with mini-hearts. 'I'm going to find LJ at break and tell him how I feel. Maybe he's like Romeo and just needs to hear me say it first before he can commit.'

It's cute the way she trails around after me. LJ's mocking conversation echoes in my head. 'You can't!' I gasp.

'Don't worry,' Savannah reassures me. 'I'm not going to say it to his face.' She lifts her jotter to reveal a folded piece of paper. 'I've written him a note.'

'Savannah Smith!' Mrs Dalton barks from her desk.

'We're trying to have a discussion here and you've talked your way through the whole lesson!'

'But I was quiet for the balcony scene!' Savannah objects.

Mrs Dalton frowns. 'That's not good enough. I want you to stay behind for break and do some extra reading.'

'Oh, Miss!' Savannah slumps back in her chair, defeated.

I give her arm a sympathetic squeeze and feel her twitch.

'Here.' Savannah thrusts the note into my lap. 'You can do it.'

I've one eye on Mrs Dalton.

She's reading from the play. '*I have no joy of this contract tonight. It is too rash, too unadvised, too sudden.*'

'Are you nuts?' I hand it back under cover of the desk.

'Please,' Savannah begs. 'You only have to slip it in his locker.'

Mrs Dalton looks up from the text. I'm scared Sav will get into more trouble for talking. I snatch the note from her hand. 'OK,' I agree through gritted teeth. 'I'll do it.'

'Are you coming, Treac?' I glance over my shoulder at her as I'm swept out of the English room in the flood of students heading for the vending machines.

'I promised I'd meet Jeff,' Treacle calls.

Savannah's note is burning holes in my fingertips. 'Can't he wait?' Now would be a good time to bring Treacle up to speed on LJ's real opinion of Savannah. Then we could decide together what to do with this note.

But Treacle's caught up in her own drama. 'He's got county try-outs this afternoon, I need to help him practise his tackling.'

It looks like I'm flying solo with the note. 'OK,' I concede gracefully. There's no need to lay a guilt trip on Treacle. I wave her goodbye and head for the lockers. I don't know why. After overhearing LJ's boy-talk yesterday, I know I'm not giving him the note. It's bound to be filled with soppy nonsense. My heart twists as I imagine LJ making fun of its contents with Mark and Harry. Poor Savannah.

Perhaps I can lose it. I could tell Savannah that someone accidentally knocked it out of my hand and it blew out of a window.

But I know she'll worry at the thought of her innermost desires fluttering around the yard.

Then I have a better idea.

I could use this note to bring her closer to Marcus.

The idea zaps me like lightning. It's so brilliant it could win an award. If I slip it into Marcus's locker instead of LJ's, he'll think Savannah has a crush on him and he might ask her out again.

It's the perfect solution.

Marcus's locker is 318. I know that because it's two down from Treacle's. The hall crowds are starting to thin out. I cross the corridor and follow the line of dented locker doors till I reach the three hundreds.

315, 316, 317.

Smiling, I slip the note through the vent at the top of 318.

'What are you doing?'

I jump at the sound of Marcus's voice behind me.

Oh no!

There *is* a God, and he hates me.

I turn round, babbling. 'Hi, Marcus. What are you doing here? I thought your locker was way over there.' I point wildly along the corridor.

'You know my locker's near Treacle's.' Marcus looks

at me like I've gone insane while he undoes the padlock.

I freeze, horror-stricken, as Savannah's note slides out and floats gently to the floor.

Marcus bends down and picks it up, looking puzzled. 'Is this from you?' He opens the paper and reads.

I'm backing away, my stomach knotting as I watch Marcus turn red.

He looks up at me, waving the note helplessly. He's turned zombie; his mouth is moving but no words are coming out. What on earth has Savannah written?

Oh God, did she sign it?

'It's not from me!' I tell him quickly. 'Someone just asked me to deliver it for them.' I keep backing away, wanting to turn and break into a sprint.

'Look, I'm sorry, Gem.' Marcus's eyes glitter with sympathy. 'I thought we'd talked about this. I'm really flattered. *Really*. You're a nice person but I just don't feel the same way.'

'It's not from me,' I practically scream. 'Honest.'

Marcus walks toward me, holding out the note. 'I can't keep this.' He stuffs it in my hand. 'I'm sorry. I'm really touched but I just can't keep it.'

My gaze darts wildly around the corridor as I try to avoid his.

With a rush of relief I spot Sam heading our way.

'Sam! Hi!' I welcome him like a long-lost friend.

'Where are you heading?' Perhaps I can go with Sam, anything to get me out of this deadly moment.

Sam slows down. 'I'm going to my form room.'

'Are you passing the vending machines? We could get a Coke or something.' *Rescue me!*

Sam looks at me like I'm crazy. 'No. Sorry, they're nowhere near.'

'Maybe we could share a Kit-Kat?' I'm begging now. Surely Sam will take the hint? He's Mr Nice Guy. But he just looks even more bewildered.

'Sorry, Gemma.' He keeps walking. 'I can't. I've got to get to class.'

Marcus shrugs apologetically then heads toward the gym.

I'm left standing beside the lockers feeling bewildered.

I unfold Savannah's note and read it.

There's no signature. Just three hideous words.

I LOVE YOU.

As the clock in the kitchen turns to eight o'clock I shrug on my blazer and stare in the hall mirror. I should wear a paper bag over my head. They do that with birds, don't they? Put hoods on them to keep them calm. Apparently, if you cover a bird's head, it thinks the world's gone away.

It should work on a bird-brain like me.

I LOVE YOU.

The words are still clanging round my head. I vow never to interfere with anyone's love life again.

'Bye, Mum,' I call as I head out the door and trudge toward the bus stop, heels dragging.

At least it was Marcus.

If anyone else had that much incriminating evidence on me, it'd be all over their Facebook page by now. Marcus's status just says: *Gone kayaking.* Perhaps that's just his way of saying: *Hiding from stalker.*

The bus is trundling towards the stop as I reach it. I stick out my thumb and steer my thoughts towards lunchtime's webzine meeting.

'Hey, Gem!' Treacle comes puffing after me as I climb

onboard. 'I've had an idea.' As I slide into a seat, she slides in beside me. 'What if I slip a note into Marcus's locker too?' she suggests. She's been fully briefed on yesterday's disaster.

'How will that help?' I hug my bag miserably. 'He'll just assume I've put you up to it and get a restraining order.'

Her eyes are sparkling with mischief. 'Not if I sign it "from Chelsea"?'

'What if he asks Chelsea about it?' I argue. 'Or catches you planting it like he caught me? What would Jeff say?' I don't want any more mix-ups. I just want Savannah and Marcus to read their horoscopes and fall in love.

It's a simple plan.

So why does it keep going wrong?

I spend the morning slouching behind desks, staring in rapt fascination at my pencil case and shuffling in and out of classrooms using Treacle as a human shield.

The one time I bump into Marcus, he gives me a sympathetic smile then drops his gaze.

'What's up, Gem?' Savannah slides one arm through mine and another through Treacle's as we head toward the dining room for lunch. 'You've hardly spoken all morning.'

'I'm just tired.' I can't tell her I delivered her love note to Marcus.

'But it's Webzine Day!' she reminds me. 'You're usually Mrs Chatty on Webzine Day.'

Treacle draws her fire. 'Have you read the new issue, Sav?'

'Of course!'

I blink at Savannah. '*All* of it?'

'Well, mainly the horoscopes,' she confesses.

I act innocent. 'So what did Jessica say this week?' I want to know if my advice has hit home.

'I think she's worried about my diet.' She gazes down at her stomach. 'Do you think I'm getting fat?'

Treacle stares at the hollow space where Savannah's belly should be. 'No.'

'Maybe that's why LJ hasn't responded to my note yet,' she sighs.

Treacle shrugs. 'Maybe he hasn't spotted it.' She catches my eye. 'Those lockers are big. It could have landed behind his sports kit or something.'

Savannah isn't convinced. 'You've seen American girls on TV.' She blows out her cheeks. 'Next to them I'm a whale.'

Treacle pops Savannah's balloon face with two fingers. 'Don't be dumb.'

'Why else did LJ tell me not to mix carbs and protein?' Savannah frowns. 'And now Jessica's telling me to lay off the cheesecake.'

'Are you sure Jessica was actually talking about food?' I ask.

153

'What did the horoscope say exactly ?' Treacle asks like she doesn't know already.

'*Stay off cheesecake and eat homegrown food.*'

'Are you sure she meant *real* cheesecake?' Treacle presses.

Before Savannah can answer we hit the lunch-room crowds and have to fight our way to our favourite table. Sally and Ryan are already there. My heart sinks as I spot Marcus sitting beside them. Savannah pulls out a chair beside him and beckons me toward it. But I'm already squeezing into a space at the other end of the table. Treacle sits beside me.

Sally waves a piece of paper, grinning. 'I've printed them out!'

Savannah grabs the A4. 'The horoscopes! What's yours?'

'*Don't talk with your mouth full, you might spit crumbs.*' Sally shrugs. 'Jessica seems to have some food issues this week.'

Or she might be gently hinting for you to gossip less. I peel the lid off my lunch box and take out an apple.

Savannah takes the chair beside Marcus and pulls a chocolate mousse from her lunch box.

Sally stares at it, horrified. 'I thought Jessica warned you to go easy on dessert?'

'Just cheesecake,' Savannah argues.

'Don't mess with Jess.' Sally gives her a warning look. 'She's never been wrong before.'

As Savannah hesitates, Sally hooks the apple from my hand, pointing excitedly at the little Union Jack sticker on the side. 'Didn't Jessica say something about home-grown food?'

Savannah's gaze swivels toward me. 'Can we swap, Gem?'

She looks so hopeful, I give in. 'OK.'

Savannah flashes me a smile and hands me her mousse while Sal rolls my apple across the table.

Marcus watches as it tumbles into Savannah's hand.

His horoscope twinkles in my head. *Don't do a Newton and worry about the gravity of the situation, sink your teeth in and enjoy.*

I watch him, breathless, hoping he's read Jessica's column. This could be the sign he needs to ask Savannah out again. His cheeks flush as Savannah puts the apple to her lips.

'Hey, Climate-Zone!'

LJ's holler makes Savannah jump. He's weaving his way toward our table. Bethany's beetling along behind him, trying to keep up.

'Nice choice of food group.' LJ glances at Savannah's apple. 'I've got an aunt who's a fruitarian. She's nearly thirty but she only looks twenty-five.' He widens his per-fect smile and moves on.

Sally whispers something in Savannah's ear and Savannah's face lights up.

'You're right!' Savannah watches LJ leave, her face glowing. 'How did Jessica know an *apple* would attract his attention? That woman is amazing.I wish I could meet her.'

My stomach lurches.

'Oh that would be so cool!' Sally sighs. 'Can't you sort something out, Gem?'

'No!' I bark, then notice the odd look that passes over Sally's face. I attempt to smile sweetly – and calmly – at Sally. 'I mean, she lives a long way away, so it's not that easy.'

'Where does she live?' Savannah immediately asks.

'I'm not sure.'

'Well how do you know it's a long way away then?' Sally says.

'Because – because – Cindy told us.' Desperate to change the subject, I make a grab for Sal's printout. 'Hey Marcus, have you read your stars?' There's no way I'm going to let this opportunity pass. '*Though it may seem hopeless, the apple of your eye is still on the tree. Stay close by and it may drop into your lap.*'

Savannah gasps. 'Quick!' She thrusts the apple back at me. 'It's your apple!' She's giving me big eyes, clearly trying to tell me to make my move.

The apple is like a hot coal in my hand. 'Here!' Panicking, I toss it to Marcus and stand up. 'I'm not hungry.' Grabbing my lunch box, I flee the room.

'Gemma!' Treacle sprints after me.

'I did it again, didn't I?' My face is burning as she catches up with me outside the lunch room.

'It did look kind of odd,' she admits. 'Though I'm not sure whether, technically, flinging fruit at your loved one is considered a seduction technique.'

'What was I meant to do?' I squeak. 'Sit and eat it in front of him?' I hold my head. 'Why didn't Savannah just eat it?'

'She was just trying to help you,' Treacle soothes.

'I know.' I shove my lunch box into my bag. 'Jessica Jupiter is an idiot. She just keeps making everything worse, not better! And now they want to *meet* her!'

Treacle gives me a squeeze. 'Don't worry,' she says. 'I'll go back and say you'd just realized you were late for your webzine meeting.'

I look at my watch. The meeting starts in five minutes. 'Thanks, Treacle.'

'Make sure you eat something.' She turns and heads back to the lunch room.

I picture the sandwiches wilting in my lunch box. I couldn't be less hungry. 'OK,' I call after her and head for webzine HQ.

'Hi, Sam.' He's the only one in the storeroom when I arrive.

He's strumming his guitar and doesn't look up. 'Hello.'

'Are you nervous about Friday's gig?'

'No, not really.' He still doesn't look up.

I take a seat behind a PC, relieved when Barbara and Cindy barge in, breaking the weird silence with chatter. I guess not everyone can be super-friendly all the time, not even Sam.

'... and now Bethany Richards is talking with an American accent.' Cindy flicks her hair back. 'She sounds like Teen-Talk Barbie.'

'I think it's sweet,' Barbara coos.

'Clearly not sweet enough for Loud Jerk.' Cindy sits on her desk and surveys the room. 'Hi, Sam.'

'Hi.' Sam's fingers are running up and down the fretboard but his eyes are fixed firmly on his strings.

As the twins file in, Cindy slides a clipboard from her bag. When Jeff arrives next, Will loping after him, she launches straight into the webzine post-mortem. 'Your school-trip-fatality piece went down well, Will. Four emails already. And all of them accusing you of being a spoil-sport.' She smiles. 'I didn't realize our readers were so smart.'

'Who cares?' Will holds up a yellow office slip. 'I think we've made the staff nervous.' He waves the bit of paper. 'I've been summoned by the Head.'

Barbara shakes her head. 'He'll be worrying about parental anxieties.'

Will sniffs. 'He'll be worrying about his insurance coverage.'

Cindy glances at her clipboard. 'Nice feedback on the earphone reviews,' she tells Phil and Dave. 'I've had two emails already asking about suppliers. Perhaps next time you could include a list in your article?'

'No problem.' David scribbles a note in his jotter.

Barbara looks at Cindy hopefully. 'Were there any comments on my *Helping Out with Chores* piece?'

'Not yet, but it's still early,' Cindy reassures her.

'I'm sure the emails will start flooding in once your fans have taken out the trash,' Will snipes.

Cindy turns on him. 'How's your *big* article going, Will? Any progress yet?' Her gaze swoops toward me. 'Have you two made any kind of breakthrough?'

I swap looks with Will and let him answer.

'We'll find out on Friday,' he tells her.

'Oh?' Cindy tips her head. 'Does that mean you'll be missing Sam's gig?'

Sam looks up sharply. 'I thought you'd bought tickets.'

Will smiles. 'And we'll be using them.' He reaches out an arm and ruffles my hair like a fond uncle. 'Won't we, Gemma?'

I shake him off.

Sam snorts and looks back down at his guitar.

'Jeff.' Cindy steers the meeting back on course. 'Miss

159

Bayliss wants me to pass on her congratulations. She thought your coverage of the Year Nine netball final was great. She's pleased to see you applying the same standards to your coverage of girls' sports as you do to boys' sports.'

Jeff leans back on his chair. 'I actually really enjoyed the game.'

Cindy makes a note on her clipboard. 'Do we all have ideas for our next pieces?'

Phil sticks up his hand excitedly. 'We're going to get to see a brand new iPhone.'

Cindy arches an eyebrow. 'Review?'

Dave grins. 'Yep.'

'Nice.' Cindy makes a note.

Barbara winds her pen through her hair. 'What do you think of a feature on the differences between US and UK schools?'

Jeff's chair clanks from two legs to four as he swings forward. 'An interview with LJ?'

Barbara nods. 'I thought it might be interesting.'

'If you can get him to stop talking about himself for long enough,' Will growls.

'You sound jealous, Will.' Cindy's eyes flash with interest. 'Is LJ stealing too much of the limelight?'

'He can have it.' Will meets her gaze. 'I'm surprised you're not basking in his glow with the rest of girls.'

I think of Savannah.

'He's not my type,' Cindy sniffs. 'Way too cheesy.'

'You should check with Jessica Jupiter,' Will scoffs. 'She's advising one twelfth of the school to lay off American cheesecake this week.'

He reads Jessica! I drop my head, grinning behind my hair.

Sam gets to his feet. 'Are we done here?'

Cindy glances at the clock. 'I guess.' As Sam makes another of his fast exits, she grabs her bag, stows her clipboard and scurries after him. 'Sam, I was wondering about Friday ...'

As they trail away down the corridor, Will grabs my arm.

'Are you ready for Friday, Stone?'

I nod. I can't wait!

'Good.' He lets go and heads for the door. 'Don't be late.'

No way! I close my eyes and wish. *Please let us find something on Wiggins!* This could be the first story of the rest of my life.

'I told Jeff to meet us at the bus stop.' Treacle peers at herself in my bedroom mirror.

It's Friday night and we're getting ready for the gig. Savannah is lolling on my bed. She's already dressed, in full emo costume, for LJ's benefit. 'It's so cool we're all going together this week.' She rolls on to her back, mirror in one hand, eyeliner in the other, and thickens the black rim of her blue-shaded eyes.

Treacle's babed up in a dusky-pink number with heels.

'You look stunning,' I tell her.

She smoothes her long, black hair then glances at my reflection. 'Is that what you're wearing?'

I'm dressed for reporting not flirting, wearing jeans and a plain top, just like last week.

'I feel comfortable in this,' I tell her.

Savannah climbs off the bed and grabs a hairbrush. 'You could at least fix your hair.' She starts bouncing my curls with deft strokes. 'It's one of your best features.'

I duck away. 'Don't make it any curlier!'

'But it's gorgeous,' Savannah argues.

I hold up my hands 'I'm fine just as I am.'

Savannah drops the brush and sighs. 'Whatever.'

By the time we're boarding the bus to Sounds, my heart is hammering so fast I can hardly breathe.

This might be the night that launches my career.

Treacle pairs off with Jeff near the front of the bus, while Savannah and I head to the back, where Sally is beckoning. As we near her, a hand grabs my wrist and pulls me down on to a seat.

It's Will, hunched beside the window, the collar of his leather jacket turned up. 'We need to stay together all night,' he tells me. 'If we see anything incriminating, we need the other one as a witness. Otherwise it's just our word against Wiggins.'

Savannah glances over her shoulder. 'Gem?'

'I'm fine here,' I tell her.

She gives me a knowing wink and squeezes in beside Sally.

I cringe as I realize what's going through her mind. Now she thinks I like Will!

Will slides a look at my hair. 'Couldn't you have worn a hat or something? I mean this whole pre-Raphaelite thing you've got going on may score points in the lunch room but, if you're working undercover, it makes you kind of easy to spot.'

Flushing, I grab a hairband from my pocket and tie my insanely wavy hair into a ponytail.

Will stares out of the window and stays silent while the bus bounces its way into town.

As it nears our stop, Savannah and Sally get up and join Jeff and Treacle as they crowd the aisle.

'Are you coming, Gem?' Savannah asks.

'Will's got my ticket,' I mutter, not even trying to explain.

Will glowers at her like the Big Bad Wolf. 'Don't worry, I won't eat her.'

Savannah swaps looks with Sal. 'I guess we'll see you in there then.'

I shrink into my jacket. I can't wait till this story gets published and I can explain to everyone why I've been hanging out with Will.

He nudges me up from the seat and we filter off the bus, hanging back as the others jostle their way into the club.

A steady drizzle sweeps the pavement. Neon lights frame the doorway of Sounds and flash in the puddles on the floor.

I follow Will to the door and wait like a trained poodle while he shows our tickets. Then we head inside.

He gazes, blinking, around the foyer like a Martian in Tesco.

'This way.' I take the lead and push through the doors

to the dance floor. Alex and Kenny are setting up on stage while the DJ pumps some Beyoncé into the room. Savannah and Sally are already making their way through the crowd, heading for LJ's gang clustered at the bar.

'Gemma!' Treacle beckons from a table at the edge of the heaving dance floor.

'I'll be there in a minute,' I mouth, pointing at my watch.

Treacle hurries over, one eye on Will. 'You're going to sit with us, right?'

'We've got a message for – er – Sam,' I nod toward the stage. 'Webzine stuff. We won't be long.'

Treacle shrugs. 'OK.' She waves at Jeff, who's sitting at the table as awkwardly as a Man U supporter in Liverpool's end of the stadium. 'I'm going to see if I can get Jeff dancing.' She disappears into the wall of sound and I turn back to Will.

He's got his hands in his jacket pocket and he's scanning the club. 'How do we get backstage?' he asks.

'This way.' I lead him to the door Sam showed me last week and we burst out of the heat and darkness into the cool breezeblock corridor.

The hairs on the back of my neck are pricking. What if Wiggins spots me? Will he remember me from last week? I suddenly wish I had worn a hat.

I glance around. The hallway's empty.

'Which way?' Will asks.

'Here.' I head down the corridor toward Sam's dressing room. The door's open and I put my finger to my lips as I lead Will past.

I can hear Sam inside, chatting to Pete. 'Ready?' he says as a guitar riff rips through the air. 'Let's go.'

'Come on!' I grab Will's arm and drag him toward the fire door. We slip through it just a moment before Sam and Pete appear from the dressing room. They're toting guitars and heading for the stage.

'Whoa!' Will's staring at the stacks of boxes lining the walls.

There are twice as many as last week.

'That delivery must have arrived,' I guess.

'I wonder what's in them.' Will jabs a box with his finger.

I'm scanning the corridor where it corners toward Wiggins's office. My ears are peeled.

In the distance I hear Sam's band crank into action. Guitars wail and drums hammer. As Sam launches into the lyric, Will pulls a box off one of the stacks. It's taped shut. He slides a bank card out of his pocket and uses it to slice through the tape. Then he pulls at the lid.

As the tape rips at one end, I hear footsteps.

Wiggins appears round the corner. His eyes pop as he spots us.

'Look out!' I grab Will's arm. A large square man steps out behind Wiggins. He looks like a shaved gorilla.

'Oi! What are you doing?' Wiggins points at us, colour flooding his big round head. His gorilla plunges past him. I swear I feel the ground shake as he pounds towards us.

'Run!' Will pushes me ahead of him and I sprint for the fire door. I barge through it, my heart busting up into my throat. I glance back, expecting to see Will at my heels, but the gorilla's got him and is pressing him up against a wall. Will's dangling from his meaty fists like a beanie-baby.

'Call the police!' Will shouts to me.

The gorilla lands a fist in Will's stomach and Will crumples.

Horrified, I flee.

I race past Sam's dressing room, blind with panic, looking for a place to shelter.

Veering left, I scale a short staircase three steps at a time and dive past a stack of speakers.

The world opens up around me in a blaze of noise and light.

I blink into spotlights. A roar erupts somewhere beyond the blinding flare.

Oh no!

I'm on stage.

Drums pound behind me. My eyes adjust. I make out

Sam hanging on to his mic, staring at me as he mouths his song.

Something hard jabs my back. I spin. Alex nods at me, grinning, and nudges me across the stage with his Fender. As I stumble backward, tripping over wires, Sam grabs a tambourine from the floor and shoves it into my hand.

'Shake it!' he hisses.

Numb with shock I start tapping the tambourine against the heel of my hand. The drums are making my head rattle and my ears are ringing from the screaming guitars. Desperate to look part of the band, I chase the beat with the tambourine, searching for the riff, so disoriented by the racket that every tap is a miss-hit. A chimpanzee would be giving a better performance.

'Gem!'

I spot Savannah, leaning over the stage waving her arms toward me. Treacle's next to her, whooping through cupped hands.

Oh great! A fan club. I grin at them inanely, my eyes swivelling as I look for an escape route.

'Tambourine solo!' Treacle roars.

Sam and Alex swap looks, then Sam nods at Kenny and Pete.

They take the noise level down by about four thousand decibels, till the hopeless rattling of my tambourine stands out like a one-man-band at a wedding.

The crowd yowl with delight as I swing the tambourine above my head and start clapping it wildly against my other hand. Savannah and Treacle are falling against each other, screaming with laughter.

I stare pleadingly at Sam. *Let me go!*

He shrugs and signals to the band with a shake of his mic and they crank up the noise once more.

Desperate to escape, I stumble across the stage and ease myself through the gap between Pete's bass and Kenny's drums.

Will's being pulped! I've got to call the police. I squeeze past Pete and head for the stage wings. Sam watches me go, still working at the mic, his face baffled.

I shrug at him apologetically and bow my way into the shadows. 'Sorry!' I mouth before I drop the tambourine and leap down a short staircase.

I crouch in the pool of shadow beside the stage and pull out my phone. My hands are shaking as I dial nine-nine-nine, swallowing panic as the voice at the other end of the line makes me go through name and number until finally I blurt: 'There're drug dealers at Sounds nightclub! They've got my friend, Will. They're going to kill him!'

As soon as the operator has all the details I terminate the call and start fighting through a jumble of wires and boxes, trying to find my way backstage again. At last I burst out into the familiar breezeblock hallway. The fire door is to my right and I creep toward it.

There's nothing but boxes in the corridor behind.

What have they done with Will?

I push open the fire door gingerly and slip through.

I hear Dave Wiggins's voice echo from around the corner.

Tiptoeing, I creep closer, then dart across the opening and duck down against the emergency exit. Leaning forward, I can see round a stack of boxes. I have a clear view along the corridor to Wiggins's office. He's standing outside while his gorilla holds Will in a vicious arm lock.

'I'll ask you again.' Wiggins leans closer to Will. 'What were you doing back here?'

Will's acting tough. 'Tell your bouncer to let go and I'll tell you.'

Wiggins nods to the gorilla, who releases Will.

'I'm with the band.' Will rubs his arm where the gorilla gripped it. 'They told me to come back here and get some snacks.' He sounds indignant.

'So you thought you'd rip off a few boxes while you were here.'

'When I couldn't find a vending machine I thought the snacks must be in the boxes.' I'm impressed. Even I'm half convinced by Will's wide-eyed act.

Young Reporters Foil Drug Baron.

I'm already writing the story in my head.

Last night, two teen journalists infiltrated a local drugs ring and uncovered the biggest haul of drugs ever found.

Wiggins is heavy-breathing in Will's face. 'Why would we keep snacks in sealed boxes?' He thumps one of the stacks crowding him.

The drug dealer, Dave Wiggins, caught one reporter and grilled him mercilessly. But the brave reporter stayed calm under questioning until his colleague raced to the rescue.

I try to imagine the article as it will appear in *The Times* and it dawns on me that I need a picture for the story.

I grab my phone, lean around the stack of boxes and click a snapshot.

'Hey, you!' Wiggins blasts me with a shout. 'It's another one!' he yells. 'They're like bloody rats!'

I back away as his gorilla lunges toward me. I jump back. The handle of the emergency exit jabs my spine. I reach back and push down hard.

It doesn't move.

It's jammed.

'Come here, you!'

As the gorilla grabs my arm I swallow back a scream.

'Get your hands off me!' Fear turns to rage as the gorilla hauls me along the corridor and parks me beside Will.

Will flashes me an apologetic look.

I stare back defiantly. He doesn't need to be sorry. I knew the risk I was taking.

'Leave us alone,' I shout at Wiggins. 'We haven't done anything!'

'Oh, really?' he sneers. 'What about my box, you little thief?' He points at the half-opened box Will left at the corner.

'We weren't stealing,' I snap. 'We wanted to see the dru—'

Will silences me with a kick. 'OK, so we thought we'd steal some of your snack stock,' he confesses. 'We were just after some crisps for the after-gig party and we figured we'd find some back here. Call the police and have us arrested!' As he gives Wiggins a challenging stare, the fire door bangs open.

There's the sound of boots stomping up the corridor. Two policemen come skidding round the corner.

'Let go of those kids!' one of them shouts.

The gorilla loosens his grip and I dart toward the police. 'He's dealing drugs!' I say, pointing at Wiggins.

'The club is just a cover.' Will grabs a box and drops it at the policeman's feet. 'Open it and see for yourselves.'

The policeman looks curious. 'Well, well, Wiggins,' he growls. 'Have you been upping your game?'

Will nudges me. 'Get a picture, Gemma.'

I flick out my camera and prepare to take a shot as the policeman bends down and tears open the box.

I click a snapshot as the police pulls something out.

Something ginger.

And hairy.

Wiggins snatches it off the policeman. 'Drugs?' He's outraged. 'What do you think I am? These are *rugs*! Not drugs?'

Rugs? I stare at the hairpiece dangling from his hand like a dead rat and my mind whirs and clicks into place. Rugs! *Wigs!* Dave Wiggins has been selling *wigs* on the side.

The policeman smiles at me. 'I'm Officer McDonald.' He nods toward his colleague. 'And this is Officer Benbow.'

Officer Benbow takes a handful of wigs from the box. 'Dave Wiggins,' he grins. '*Rug*-lord.' He slides a note-book from his pocket. 'Where exactly did you purchase these wigs, Mr Wiggins?'

Wiggins backs away. 'I can explain.'

'Have you got receipts?' Officer McDonald blocks the gorilla as he tries to sidle away.

'I've lost them,' Wiggins mumbles.

'Well, well, well.' Officer McDonald takes off his helmet.

Officer Benbow taps his notebook. 'We had a report of a warehouse raid last month. Apparently the haul included a shipment of wigs.'

I snap another photo as he closes in on Wiggins.

Will puts his hand on my shoulder and steers me away. 'Go on, Gemma,' he says gently. 'I'll give our evidence to the policemen. You might as well keep out of it.'

I glance at Officer McDonald.

'It's just paperwork from now on, love,' he tells me. 'You go back to the gig.'

Paperwork? I feel disappointed. As adrenaline stops swamping my thoughts, I realize that our huge drugs bust has turned out to be petty theft.

The policeman holds out his hand. 'Thanks for the tip-off, love.'

I shake it and smile. I guess it's not bad for a first case.

I'm trembling as I push through the fire door and head back to the dance floor. I let the music and warmth warp around me while I deep-breathe my way back to calmness. Then I scan the crowd for Treacle and Savannah.

LJ and his crowd are still hanging by the bar, but there's no sign of Savannah. And the table where Treacle and Jeff were sitting is filled with other kids. I weave through the crowd till I bump into Sally.

She jumps like I stood on her tail. 'Gemma!' Her greeting is bright – and guilty. Like I've just caught her copying my homework.

'Where's Sav?'

She glances toward the entrance. 'Dunno.'

I'm suspicious, but I don't question her. Instead I follow her nervous gaze and push through the door into the foyer.

Savannah and Marcus are huddled in a corner. Savannah's head is bowed on to Marcus's shoulder. As Marcus spots me he murmurs something into her ear.

Savannah snaps away from Marcus like he's on fire. 'Hi, Gem!' she cries in the same über-bright voice as Sal.

'What's up?' I ask. As usual I start guessing headlines. *Schoolgirls in Nightclub Cover-up. Teens Caught in Dance-floor Shocker.*

'You look like you've murdered Treacle and are trying to hide the body,' I joke.

Savannah pulls a guilty face. 'It's worse than that.' She steers me away from Marcus.

'You sold her to the Russian mafia?' I'm trying to keep joking, but the serious look on Savannah's face is starting to worry me.

She whimpers pitifully. 'OhGodohGodohGod!' She's jabbing her finger into her temples like her brain's trying to escape.

'What?' I can't stand it any longer.

'I'm soooooo sorry,' Savannah whines. 'Please don't kill me.'

'I will if you don't tell me what's going on.'

Marcus is looking shifty in the corner. Is he her accomplice?

Savannah pulls in a deep breath and lets it out slowly.

'What's the matter, Savannah?'

She blabbers it out in a rush. 'I'vefallenforMaracusand hekindoffeelsthesamewayaboutme.'

Fortunately, I speak fluent Savannese. I translate into Slow-speak. 'You've fallen for Marcus and he feels the same way about you.'

She nods wretchedly. 'I'm *really* sorry, Gem. I know you like him but it was just like ... he suddenly ... and I ...' She covers her mouth with her hands. 'I'm *so* sorry.' The words are muffled by her fingertips.

I'm jubilant. It's all I can do not to run a winning circuit round the foyer. I stand there grinning like an idiot while Savannah slips into Super-explanation Mode.

'You see, Gem. I overhead LJ talking to his friends and he was *making fun* of me.'

My smile dies.

'I know,' she says seriously. 'He was actually making fun of me because I liked him. He was talking like I was a pre-schooler or something and I was just so upset.' Her eyes start brimming at the memory. She flashes them toward Marcus. 'And he was *so* kind.'

'Who? Marcus?'

'Well, duh!' Savannah gives me an idiot look. 'Did you think I meant LJ? He's, like, the *opposite* of kind. He's horrible. I don't know what I ever saw in him. I can't believe Jessica Jupiter was right again. I shouldn't have been chasing the American Dream when I've got a perfect English Muffin right in front of my eyes.' She gazes goofily at Marcus, who blushes. Then she remembers the terrible crime she's committed.

'Oh God, Gem. I'm sooooooo sorry.'

I hug her. 'You idiot.'

She looks at me, stunned.

'Do you remember I told you I wasn't interested in Marcus?' I tell her.

She nods dumbly.

'That's because I wasn't interested in Marcus.'

'Really?' She's catching up. 'But why not? He's wonderful!'

'I know.' I gently turn her round and push her toward

him. 'You're wonderful too, Sav. You're made for each other.'

She sighs happily as she melts into his arms. 'We're a match made in heaven.'

Marcus winks at me. 'Thanks for being cool about it, Gemma.'

'No problem.' I watch them wander dreamily out of the club.

'Are you coming?' Sav calls over her shoulder.

'I want to find Treacle.' I wave them away, feeling like a mother hen marrying off another chick.

I feel so happy all of a sudden I want to swing from the glitter ball. Jessica is a brilliant matchmaker and I'm a fabulous journalist. So what if it was wigs not drugs; I still helped to nail a bent businessman. Not bad for a first assignment.

'Gemma!' Treacle blares like a foghorn behind me. '*There* you are!' The door to the dance floor is still swinging as she bursts from it, Jeff on her tail. 'You were *brilliant!*'

My brain wheel-spins, trying to catch up. Has she found out about the Wiggins story already? How did she know it was me who unmasked his dodgy scam?

'I was so psyched when you came out on the stage!' Treacle hangs off my arm. 'With the tambourine? You were great! I didn't know you were part of the band! How did that happen?'

I thread my arm through hers. 'It's a long story.'

Jeff jumps ahead and opens the door for us as we head out into the night. Savannah and Marcus are already at the bus stop, nuzzling each other like shy deer.

'What's that all about?' Treacle gasps.

I tug her arm. 'You really need to keep up, Treacle,' I laugh. 'Things move fast round here.'

20

I fly through Double Maths on Monday afternoon. I can't wait to get to the editorial meeting and bask in the glory of our scoop. I mailed Will the photos I'd snapped and my notes and he wrote up the article. It'll have hit Cindy's inbox by now.

My mind is buzzing with questions. What if the story is picked up by the local newspaper? What if it goes national?

My imagination takes over. Suddenly, I'm back in the London newsroom, waiting for the call. *Gemma Stone, youngest ever winner of the World News Prize.*

Mr Baxter's voice cuts into my thoughts. 'Gemma, have you finished?'

I pick up my pen and flip the page in my text book. 'Nearly.' I've still got five problems to solve and the clock's ticking closer to the end of lesson.

Fortunately my brain's on high-speed. I've worked through them by the time the bell rings.

Close book. Stuff bag. On my feet.

'I'll phone you this evening!' I call over my shoulder

as I leave Savannah and Treacle still packing and race to webzine HQ.

Will's already there, slapping printed copies of our article on to each desk. His leather jacket's hanging off the back of his chair and he's stripped to his shirt sleeves, acting like this happens every day.

'How does it look?' I pick up a copy, thrilled to see our work in black-and-white.

'Not bad.' Will drops the rest of his stack on Cindy's desk and slides into his seat.

Rugs Bust at Local Club by Will Bold.

My name's not next to his. I feel a stab of disappointment. Maybe it was too much to expect a byline on my first story.

A raid on Sounds nightclub on Friday night uncovered a haul of stolen goods.

There's my photo of PC Benbow holding a hairpiece, Wiggins in the background looking like a kid who just got busted stealing from his mother's purse.

A consignment of wigs was discovered by reporter Will Bold in a tense undercover investigation. And when police raided the nightclub after Bold's tip-off, the wigs turned out to be just the tip of the iceberg.

Sam enters the room, slides his backpack on to the floor and starts browsing through the article.

Almost one hundred car sat-navs and a host of other

electrical goods were seized from backstage at the club during
a performance by local band Hardwired.

'Thanks for the mention, Will,' Sam says, leaning back in his chair.

Will runs his hand through his hair. 'No problem.'

I'm still waiting for my mention. After all, it was me who overheard the first dodgy phone call and who dialled the police while Will was getting tenderized by the gorilla.

After the raid, officers filled dozens of evidence bags with
the suspected stolen items. Two men aged fifty-five and thirty-
two were arrested on suspicion of handling stolen goods and
later released on police bail pending further enquiries.

Is that it? Where's my name? I look at Will. He's looking very pleased with himself.

'Thanks for the email, Will. It's a good story.' Cindy strides in and sits on her desk. She lifts the stack of articles Will's left there and fans herself with them.

Will smiles smugly. 'Worth waiting for?' He's clearly going to get as much mileage here as he can.

'Will.' Cindy leans forward and gives him the long-lashed look she normally saves for Sam. 'You're a genius.' She keeps her gaze fixed on him as she beckons Barbara, Phil and Dave through the door. 'I don't know what the webzine would do without you. We owe our very existence to your courage and integrity. You are now, and will for ever be, my *hero*.' With a flick of her perfect hair, she snaps back into Ice Queen mode and addresses the rest of us. 'Anyone else want to massage Will's ego?' she asks. 'I've only got one pair of hands.'

Will scowls at her as Jeff walks in and sits down.

'What have I missed?' Jeff asks.

Sam fills him in. 'Will's being smug. Cindy's cutting him down to size.'

Jeff drags his chair forward. 'Same as usual then.'

Cindy takes control. 'It is a good scoop,' she concedes. 'And the local paper are picking up the story, which is a real boost for the webzine.'

I've made the local paper!

Except I haven't.

I slump in my chair.

My name's not mentioned anywhere.

Mr Harris swings in. 'Congratulations!' He's eyes are shining. 'Brilliant story, Will.'

'I worked on it too,' I snap.

Mr Harris looks round like he's searching for mice, then spots me. 'Oh, Gemma! Is this the piece you were helping out with?' He smiles indulgently. 'You must be really pleased it turned out so well.'

I was the first one on the scene! Isn't anyone going to mention that? I decide to blow my own trumpet. 'I was there, you know. When they arrested Wiggins!'

Mr Harris frowns. 'At the club?'

'During the raid,' I tell him.

Mr Harris frowns harder. 'I don't want you putting yourself at risk. I don't want any students getting into trouble because of this webzine.' He turns to Will. 'I hope you were looking after Gemma at the club.'

'Of course.' Will reassures Mr Harris. 'I made sure she didn't get in anyone's way.'

'You're right, Mr Harris.' Cindy chimes in. 'Perhaps it's safer to keep Gemma reviewing beauty products in future.'

I stare at the gruesome twosome as they suck up to Mr H. I know exactly what they're doing. Will can't bear to admit he had help making his big story. Cindy wants me to stay as her secret horoscope writer.

Cindy heaves her bag on to her lap. 'Why don't we keep this meeting short?' She's eyeing Mr Harris. 'We can go over our stories at Wednesday's meeting.'

Yeah. When Mr Harris isn't here and you're in charge.

'Sounds good to me.' Will's on his feet and following Mr Harris out of the door before I've finished riding the rest of Cindy's thought-wave.

Barbara and Cindy follow them.

Jeff exits, flashing comic books at the twins. 'Can you believe Hypno-Hustler tries to get the cops to protect him against Spider-Man?'

I stare after them, feeling like I've been mugged in broad daylight.

'So you saw the raid?'

Sam's still in the room.

I blink at him. 'Yes.'

'Wow.' He leans back on his desk. 'That must have been scary.'

'It was exciting.' I stare at my shoes, suddenly self-conscious. '*And* a bit scary. I thought they were drug dealers. When the bouncer grabbed Will I thought we were dead. I'm just glad I got away long enough to phone the police.'

'*You* phoned the police?'

'Yeah.' I look at him. 'I'd overheard Wiggins making a deal on the phone that week you showed me backstage.'

'*Backstage*!' Sam looks like he's doing sums in his head. '*That's* why you wanted to see backstage.'

'Yeah.' I wind a strand of hair round my finger. 'I hope you don't mind. Will asked me to look around and when I heard Wiggins making dodgy phone calls, we came back to investigate.'

'So *that's* why you were with Will!' Sam's eyes light up. 'You were working on a story with him?'

'Duh!' I use Savannah's idiot look. 'Did you think I was enjoying his company?'

'He's not so bad,' Sam says generously.

'Try being a Year Nine girl when he's around.'

'Do I have to?'

I laugh. 'No.'

'I enjoyed your performance, by the way,' Sam says, as he tugs his bag off the desk.

'Performance?' It takes me a moment to catch up. 'Oh on stage!' In all the excitement of the article I'd almost forgotten my impromptu tambourine solo. I shrivel into my blazer. 'Sorry about that,' I murmur. 'I was hiding from the bouncer.'

'Interesting place to hide.' He hooks his bag on to his shoulder.

I hear the crowd laughing in my head and cringe even more. 'Don't worry, I think I'll leave the music scene to you in future.'

'Shame.' Sam holds the door open for me.

I slip past him and head into the hallway. 'Why?'

'I've got two tickets to the Spider Monkeys gig this weekend and I was wondering if you'd like to come with me.' He avoids my gaze.

'OK,' I tell him. I feel suddenly happy. 'I'd love to.'

We head out into the hallway.

'Great.' Sam flicks off the light and closes the door behind us. 'I'll pick you up on Saturday at seven.'

'Sam asked you *out?*' Savannah nearly drops her purse.

I've just dropped the Spider Monkeys bomb. 'It's not a date or anything,' I tell her quickly.

Treacle nudges me. 'Are you sure?'

I'm queuing for popcorn with Savannah and Treacle at the cinema multiplex. It's Thursday night and Savannah has set her heart on seeing the latest sappy rom-com. Marcus and Jeff are here too and I feel like the only singleton in a kingdom of couples. I'm walking the line between spinster-aunt chaperone and independent young woman, too cool to need a boyfriend. I wasn't sure whether to come but they had begged.

'It won't be the same without you, Gem,' Treacle had pleaded with me.

'You're the third musketeer,' Savannah added.

'More like the third wheel,' I muttered.

I'd consulted Mum about whether to go.

'They asked you,' Mum had said. 'So go.'

'They were just being polite,' I argued.

Ben had chimed in too. 'Treacle and Savannah are your friends. You have to go.'

So here I am, feeling like the odd one out.

I scan the foyer, wondering who designs the carpet pattern for cinemas. I decide it's someone who hates cinemas. Or carpets.

Marcus and Jeff are hanging out by a pillar. Jeff's gazing wistfully at a movie poster. It's a three-metre high picture of an iron-jawed soldier framed by an exploding tank. MEGABOMBER – *the action will blow you away!* Marcus is staring at the ground with the sad look of a dog waiting outside a supermarket. I'm guessing that a rom-com is not his idea of a 'must-see' film.

I check my watch. Ten minutes before the film starts.

'It *has* to be a date,' Savannah insists.

I tuck a stray tendril of hair behind my ear. 'There's no way he'd ask me on a date when he's got Cindy.'

'But he's not dating Cindy,' Savannah points out.

'Not *yet.*' I picture the way Cindy looks at Sam. Like a cat watching a goldfish bowl, waiting for the shiny fish to get close enough to the surface to catch without getting her paws wet.

'Why didn't he ask *her* to the Spider Monkey gig, then?' Sav shuffles forward with the queue.

The smell of hotdogs is making my stomach growl. 'You can't talk at a gig. It's just music and crowds and you can hardly see anything except the band on stage. He'd probably take Cindy out somewhere quiet and candlelit. Somewhere intimate he could get to know her.' I see them at a table in a restaurant. Linen table-cloths, soft lighting, a waiter hovering politely. They glow – blonde, good-looking, too close to a Coke ad to be real.

Treacle rubs her nose. 'I see what you're saying, Gem. A gig isn't exactly romantic but—'

I interrupt before she tries to raise my hopes. 'He just wants someone to watch the gig with. It's probably an assignment for the webzine.'

'Are you saying he just wants editorial backup?' Savannah's eyebrows arch. 'Are you going to hold his notebook?' She's still trying to understand what I actually do on the webzine. 'Sharpen his pencils?'

I avoid the question. 'I guess he goes to so many gigs he's running out of gig-buddies.'

Treacle tugs my hair. 'Gem-*ma*!' she says crossly. 'Why are you trying to persuade us – and yourself – that he's only asked you out because you're the last person on earth?' She looks me up and down. 'Why wouldn't he want to date you?'

Savannah nods vigorously. 'You have gorgeous hair. You've got that pretty-but-don't-know-it vibe, which is always a *major* turn-on for boys. *Of course* it's a date.'

Hope fizzes. For a second I believe that Sam Baynham,

the nicest, coolest, fittest guy in Year Ten wants to date me, Gemma Stone. Jessica Jupiter's whispering in my ear: *Darling, stop playing wallflower. If you want him to act sweet, give the boy some sugar and stir.* I huff her out of my thoughts. 'Can we change the subject?'

We reach the counter.

'Next.' A twenty-foot beanpole is behind it. He's straight up and down, except for the Adam's apple bulging in his throat. He eyes us wearily. 'What do you want?'

'Two medium Cokes, one Evian and two raspberry slushies, please.' Savannah flaps her lashes, leaning across the counter eagerly, as though meeting a human beanpole is the highlight of her week. 'Two large popcorns, regular nachos, a bag of M&Ms and a hotdog.' She glances at me. 'Onions?'

'Of course.' There's one major advantage to being boyfriendless: I can choose whatever hotdog toppings I like. 'And relish and ketchup.' Treacle and Savannah daren't eat anything that might taint a kiss. I could eat raw garlic and no one would mind.

Savannah starts passing drinks and popcorn back to me till my arms are full. Then she loads up Treacle and pays the beanpole. She's holding my hotdog like it's a grenade. 'How can you eat this trash, Gem?' She swaps it for the tub of popcorn I'm holding. 'You know you're eating nothing but ears and noses, don't you?'

'Ears and noses taste great.' I take a bite, giving myself a ketchup moustache.

Jeff's heading toward us, Marcus behind him. He relieves Treacle of her snack burden. Marcus takes the popcorn from Savannah.

'Who wanted what?' Savannah runs cinema trips like the Vice President of Cinema Trips Incorporated. Without listening for an answer, she starts swapping snacks and drinks until everyone's holding their dream treat. 'Tickets.' She whips five out of her pocket and gives two to Marcus.

He looks at them, confused. 'These say *MegaBomber*.'

'Uh-huh.' Savannah touches his cheek. 'You didn't actually think I was going to make you boys sit through *Hearts Over Manhattan*, did you?' She pouts prettily, giving Marcus big eyes and cute voice. 'You must think I'm a terrible monster.'

Marcus melts. 'Thanks, Sav.'

Jeff takes his *MegaBomber* ticket and glances at Treacle. 'You're OK with seeing separate movies?'

Treacle, arms hugging a bucket of popcorn, kicks his shin. 'Duh!' She grins. 'We need some serious girl-time. Besides, you totally wouldn't get *Hearts Over Manhattan*. It's a chick-flick. They speak in code. You'd need sub-titles.'

Jeff grabs a handful of her popcorn. 'What code?'

'"I hate you" means "I love you",' Savannah explains.

191

'And "I love you" means "You're just back-up, I actually love that really handsome guy I bumped into this morning while picking up my mail".'

Marcus looks alarmed. 'Is it like that in real life?'

Savannah throws her arm round his shoulders. 'Aww,' she sympathizes. 'No. If I ever tell you I hate you, it's because I hate you.'

Jeff sneaks a grin. 'And what if you tell him you love him?'

Savannah runs her finger under Marcus's chin. 'Then he'll be a very lucky boy.' She starts to turn on her pink kitten heels then freezes. Her dismayed gaze fixes on the entrance. 'Looks like you were right, Gem.'

Sam's holding the door open for Cindy, who sweeps in, Barbara scuttling after her.

Treacle nearly spills her slushie. 'She takes Barbara on *dates?*' She moves in close to me, like we're lining up for battle. 'Mind you, we don't *know* it's a date.'

Yeah, right. Cindy's gorgeous in tight jeans and Sam's hair is gelled to perfection.

He's heading towards us. I'm suddenly hideously aware of my hotdog. Nose-based snacks are not cool. I sidle toward a bin and drop it in, then wipe off my ketchup moustache.

'Hi.' Sam greets Jeff first but his eyes are fixed on my face.

I freeze like I'm caught in the crosshairs of a sniper.

Cindy catches up. 'Hi, Jeff.' She doesn't look at us. 'What's with the child-minding?' *Now* she looks at us. 'Shouldn't you have help? That's a lot of Year Nines to handle alone.'

Treacle scowls. 'We can handle ourselves, thanks.'

Jeff puts his arm round Treacle's shoulders. 'It's just Year Ten humour. Take no notice.'

Barbara wades bravely in. 'Oh Cindy!' She laughs lightly. 'You are such a tease.'

I wonder why everyone's making excuses for the Ice Queen. Perhaps Year Tens sign oaths of loyalty at the start of every term.

Sam's still staring at me. Then he breaks away suddenly. 'What film are we watching, Cindy?'

'Don't ask me.' Cindy eyes the entrance crossly. 'This was Will's idea.'

I turn in time to see Will pushing his way through the front doors. He comes at us, crossing the foyer with giant strides. 'Have you got the tickets yet?'

Cindy glares at him. 'We don't even know what film we're going to watch.'

'I told you,' Will growls. 'It's art-house night. This is probably the only chance you'll ever get to see *The Battleship Potemkin*.'

Sam's eyes light up. 'It's a war film?'

'Silent classic made in 1925 by Eisenstein,' Will corrects him.

Jeff glances at Sam sympathetically. 'Do you want to come and see *MegaBomber* with us?' He shrugs at Will. 'Sorry, mate. I like my explosions with sound.'

Will gives us the look he must save for the chimp enclosure at the zoo. I bet he goes there every week to gloat. I imagine him shouting through the fence. 'Call yourselves evolved just because you've got opposable thumbs?' Then he shows them his iPod. 'Well, oppose *this*.'

I flip back into reality.

'Are you all going to watch *MegaBomber*?' Sam asks me. 'No, we're leaving the boys to it and watching the chick flick that's showing at the same time,' I reply. A look flashes across Sam's face, but before I can work out what it means it's gone.

Will's staring at Cindy. 'I suppose you want to watch the chick-flick?'

'Why? Because I'm blonde? Does that automatically mean I must be an airhead?' she retorts.

Sam grins. 'I don't mind admitting I'm an airhead.' He takes a tenner from his pocket. 'Anyone else for *MegaBomber*?'

Will, Cindy and Barbara shake their heads.

Sam looks at Jeff. 'So you don't mind if I tag along with you?'

'Course not.' He thumps Marcus on the shoulder. 'This is Marcus, by the way.'

'Hey, you're in Gemma's class, right?' Sam flicks his hair from his eyes.

'Yeah.' Marcus stuffs his hands in his pockets.

Savannah lifts her chin. 'He's my date,' she announces proudly.

'Lucky guy.' As Sam says and then heads for the ticket counter, Cindy stares after him.

Will steps into her line of sight. 'So it's Eisenstein for us Cinders?'

'Of course,' Cindy snaps. 'I'll get the tickets.' She heads after Sam.

Barbara chases after her. 'Cindy!'

Will unzips his leather jacket. 'She's just trying to impress me,' he grunts.

'Or *you're* trying to impress *her*,' I mutter under my breath.

'What?' He fixes me with one of his killer stares.

I fire it back at him. Rage is welling in my chest. 'What's with the art-house, Will?' I still haven't forgiven him for taking my byline. 'Are you looking for ideas to steal?'

Will sticks a hand in his back pocket. 'If you respect the artist, it's not stealing; it's *homage*.'

'*Homage*?' Savannah frowns. 'Is that, like, a breakfast cereal?'

Treacle laughs. 'Come on.' She hooks her arm through mine and Sav's. 'Lets grab some good seats.

We head for the stairs leading to Screen Five.

'Wait for me!' Barbara races after us.

I halt, stunned. '*What?*'

'I'm coming to watch *Hearts Over Manhattan*,' she puffs.

'What about Cindy?' I search the foyer behind her. Cindy's hovering beside Will at the ticket booth.

'She wants to see that silent film.' Barbara loops her handbag further up her shoulder. 'I'm scared I'll fall asleep in the middle and start snoring.'

I'm impressed. Barbara's decided to fly solo. 'Come on, then.' I lead the way.

'Have fun, boys,' Savannah shouts to Jeff and Marcus over her shoulder.

'Gemma!' Jeff calls after me. 'Wipe off your ketchup goatee.' He points to his chin.

I turn to stone as I touch mine and feel a cold, wet blob of relish. It must have been there the whole time. No wonder Sam was staring at me.

Mortified, I wipe it off and then catch up with Treacle. 'Why didn't you tell me I was wearing half my hotdog?'

'You looked kind of cute.' She throws me a mischievous smile as we push through the double doors into the darkness. 'And from the way he was looking at you, I reckon Sam thought so too.'

Read on for a sneak peek
of the next book in the series...

SiGNS of Love

Jeff opens the door to the storeroom and lets me through. This is the webzine's HQ. The friendly janitor cleared out most of the junk and set up six PCs on six ancient desks. There are still shelves of aging textbooks and glue pots lining the walls, and dust drifts down from an ancient lampshade hanging from a cracked ceiling, but I love the smell of crumbling wood and old paper. It's kind of romantic. Like being in one of the old movies Mum watches when she gets a spare moment.

Cindy and Barbara are already here. Best friends since playgroup, they look like before-and-after photos – Barbara dresses like a Maths teacher and Cindy is cutting edge, sleek as the cover of *Vogue*.

'Hi, Gemma,' Barbara smiles at me warmly and I feel instantly guilty for my internal bitch-fest. Barbara's actually really nice and, even though she writes the world's most boring feature articles while I'm stuck shrinking freckles for Cindy (Barbara's last offering: *School Uniform – Why Smarter is Better*), she never apologizes for being exactly who she is and I really admire that.

'Hi, Barbara,' I give her a small wave, feeling contrite, and shuffle behind a desk.

As I'm sliding into my seat, David and Phil Senior arrive. They're twins and they're OK. Kinda geek without the chic, but nice. They review gadgets and computer games for the webzine and they're mad about graphic novels (which I always thought were just comics, but apparently I'm wrong). Straight away they're showing one to Jeff, flipping through pages to show him the latest thrilling instalment of Cosmic Man or Blasto Boy or whatever.

The door swings open and Will blows in, the buckles on his leather jacket swinging. He sweeps his mop of dark brown hair away from his face and his smooth jaw and chiselled cheekbones catch the light. He's a good-looking package but he should wear a warning sign: *contents may offend.*

'Hi, Will,' Cindy barely looks up from her clipboard. 'Have you got another scoop for us?' She's using her couldn't-care-less voice.

'I'm working on it.' Will slouches into the seat behind his favourite PC – it's got the fastest processor in the room and he's unofficially made it his own. I silently stick another imaginary pin in his imaginary heart and wait for him to clutch his chest and fall off his chair. He doesn't. Instead he drops his book bag on the floor and stretches his long legs under his desk so his feet stick out the front.

Cindy glances at his size twelve biker boots. 'Health and safety, Will,' she chides.

'Don't worry, Cinders,' Will says acidly. 'If you trip, I promise I'll catch you before you hit the floor.'

'I'd rather hit the floor.'

'I'm not sure the floor could handle it.'

Cindy meets his eye. 'And *you* could?'

'Bickering again?' Sam's voice makes me jump. He's standing in the doorway watching Will and Cindy fight. There's a strange gleam in his eye. Is he jealous of the sparks crackling between them?

He dumps his bag on the desk beside Cindy's and sits down. 'Don't stop for me.' He glances at Cindy from under his shaggy blond fringe. 'I don't want to interrupt.'

'You're not interrupting, Sam,' Cindy tells him sweetly. 'We were just waiting for you so we could start the meeting.'

I roll my eyes. Cindy's been buzzing around Sam since the webzine started. And now it looks like he's finally getting a taste for her honey.

'Thanks, Cindy,' he mumbles and stares at his hands.

She taps her clipboard with her pen and looks brightly around the room. 'Once again, it was lovely to see my Inbox full.'

'I'll bet,' Will mutters.

'You've all submitted your articles, which I absolutely love.' She's not looking at me even though my horoscopes are one of the most popular features in the webzine. 'Why don't we quickly go over them in case I've missed something and them we can all go to lunch.'

David shoots up his hand. 'Was it OK to make our whole feature about *Call of Duty* tips and tricks?'

Sam shakes his hair out of his eyes. 'That's fine by me. I can do with the help.'

Cindy cracks a wide smile. 'Of course it is, David. I totally trust your judgment.'

Barbara slides David a look that takes me by surprise. There's a gooiness in her gaze I've never seen before.

'Barbara,' Cindy turns her laser-beam attention-ray on to her best friend. 'Thank you for submitting another fabulous article.'

Will slouches lower on his chair. 'What's this week's revelation?'

Barbara lifts her chin proudly, '*Detention: The Punishment that Keeps on Giving.*'

Will grunts, 'Giving what? Overtime to teachers?'

Barbara doesn't flinch. 'Breathing space,' she tells him. 'A quiet time to reconsider and work on improving oneself.'

'You've outdone yourself, Babs,' Will snorts.

I fight the urge to suggest he volunteers for a few weeks' detention. He could do with improving and we all need the breathing space.

'I think Barbara's come up with an interesting point of view,' David chips in. 'I can't wait to read it.'

Barbara smiles at him, a soft blush pinking her cheeks.

My romance detector starts flashing. Are there actually sparks flying in the storeroom that *aren't* directed at Cindy? I quickly slide my jotter from my bag and scribble a note. *Find out David's star sign.* Suddenly, Jessica Jupiter has a new match-making project. Maybe – with a well-worded prediction or two – she can bring David and Barbara together.

And who knows? With Barbara in love, her articles might heat up and start bubbling with interest. I'll be doing the whole school a favour . . .